Jessica straighte_____e
fluttering in her h_____r
approaching, he immediately stood up, a grin lighting his face.

"Hi, Devon," she said huskily.

"Hi, yourself," Devon returned with just a hint of seduction.

He put his arms around her and pulled her close. Jessica was in sheer bliss.

She returned the embrace, wrapping her arms around his neck. She smelled a hint of cologne on his neck and inhaled deeply. Not too strong or fragrant, just clean, fresh, and masculine. Jessica savored the moment, taking in every detail. His soft hair brushing against her cheek, the noise of his leather jacket as he moved, the soft fabric of his T-shirt. Her night with Devon was finally here.

"I knew you'd come, Elizabeth," he breathed into her ear, still holding her tight. "I knew you couldn't stay away."

Visit the Official Sweet Valley Web Site on the Internet at:

http://www.sweetvalley.com

WHAT JESSICA WANTS . . .

Written by
Kate William

Created by
FRANCINE PASCAL

BANTAM BOOKS
NEW YORK·TORONTO·LONDON·SYDNEY·AUCKLAND

RL 6, age 12 and up

WHAT JESSICA WANTS . . .
A Bantam Book / March 1998

Sweet Valley High® is a registered trademark of Francine Pascal.
Conceived by Francine Pascal.
Produced by Daniel Weiss Associates, Inc.
33 West 17th Street
New York, NY 10011.
Cover photography by Michael Segal.

ISBN: 0-553-49228-4

Published simultaneously in the United States and Canada

Bantam Books are published by Bantam Books, a division of Bantam Doubleday Dell Publishing Group, Inc. Its trademark, consisting of the words "Bantam Books" and the portrayal of a rooster, is Registered in U.S. Patent and Trademark Office and in other countries. Marca Registrada. Bantam Books, 1540 Broadway, New York, New York 10036.

PRINTED IN THE UNITED STATES OF AMERICA

OPM   0 9 8 7 6 5 4 3 2 1

To Danielle Pallotta

Chapter 1

Seventeen-year-old Devon Whitelaw pulled his Harley-Davidson Sportster into the parking lot in front of Sweet Valley High. He looked up and smiled as a couple of students ran through the front doors of the school, wearing shorts and T-shirts.

"I'm certainly not in Connecticut anymore," he said to himself as he removed his helmet and hung it on a handlebar.

The weather back in Devon's old hometown would be crisp at this time of year, but the climate in Sweet Valley was much milder, to say the least.

It was Friday afternoon, and after taking a week to relax and get used to his new town, Devon had decided to ride over to his new high school to register for classes. He had left the East Coast over a month ago when his parents had been killed in a car accident. His father's will had stipulated that Devon was required to find a guardian in order to receive his significant inheritance. After a long, sometimes heartbreaking, search Devon had found a home in Sweet Valley with the nanny from his childhood, Nan Johnstone.

Devon felt the warm sun through his faded blue jeans, and the light breeze made his cotton T-shirt ripple underneath his leather jacket. He took a deep breath of the clean salt-scented California air and sighed. For the first time in years he was beginning to believe that things were actually getting better for him. Nan's house was already more of a home to him than his parents' mansion had ever been. In fact, he was starting to feel like he had been living there for months instead of a few days.

Devon looked over his new school. It was a beautiful brick building with marble columns at the main entrance. The campus was surrounded by trees, and the grounds were immaculate. Flowers lined the paved walkways, giving the landscape a bright and cheery look. It was homey—not industrial like a lot of high schools Devon had seen. He took in every detail of his surroundings, hoping that the inside of the school would be just as welcoming.

He ascended the wide concrete steps slowly and paused before opening the tall wooden door, running a hand through his wavy brown hair. *This is it,* he thought, *my chance to start fresh.* He wasn't nervous, but he did want to savor the experience. He was about to begin a new life, and he wanted to remember every minute.

Devon swung open the door just as the bell rang, and the hall was instantly flooded with bodies. Devon was surprised at first as kids laughed and chattered all around him. But he got his bearings quickly and immediately started searching the crowd, trying to catch a glimpse of the beautiful blond girl he had spotted at last week's football game.

On a whim, Devon had attended the big match the week before, hoping to get a feel for his new school. But soon after he had arrived, he hadn't been thinking about classes and school spirit at all. He had seen the girl of his dreams walking along by the bleachers, chatting with a friend. Devon had tried to catch up with her but had lost her in the crowd. Moments later she had appeared on the track, wearing a red-and-white uniform and leading the crowd in a cheer. Devon hadn't been able to take his eyes off her at the time, and he hadn't stopped thinking about her since.

Devon saw a flash of blond hair and was about

to check it out when he felt a sudden push from behind that jolted him forward a few steps. He spun around, instinctively clenching his fists, but the person standing there wasn't at all intimidating. He was tall and lanky with tousled brown hair. A flurry of papers was falling around him as he looked nervously at Devon, smiling weakly.

"Oh, my gosh, I'm really sorry," the guy apologized quickly, his voice cracking as he spoke. "I was trying to finish a scene in this play." He held up a copy of *Macbeth*. "We're having a quiz in English today, and I'm a little behind in the reading."

Devon opened his mouth to respond, but the guy continued to ramble.

"I thought I was watching where I was going, but when I looked up—bam—there you were. I tried to avoid you, but . . ." He finished the sentence with a shrug and a helpless look.

"Hey, it's no problem," Devon said finally. The guy crouched to the floor to gather his belongings. When he reached for his calculator, which had already been kicked twice, a girl in high heels stepped on his fingers.

"Ouch!" he exclaimed, jerking back his hand and shaking it. He glanced up at Devon and grimaced. "Sometimes I can be such a klutz."

"I noticed," Devon said with a good-natured smile, kneeling down as well. The boy grinned sheepishly at Devon once more, then gathered a brown lunch bag and a stray apple up in his arms.

Devon picked up the remaining papers and pens and then helped the boy move from the center of the corridor to the side so that he could get organized.

"Jeez, thanks a lot," the boy gushed as Devon handed him the rest of his things. "I really appreciate it. Especially after I nearly knocked you over and everything."

"Don't sweat it," Devon reassured him with a casual nod. Then he smiled. "I habitually run into people myself. I find it's a great way to make new acquaintances."

"Well, if you don't already know who I am, then you must be new around here," the guy said, tucking a pen behind his ear.

"Why's that? Are you famous or something?" Devon asked.

"Official class clown at your service," the guy said, straightening up and giving a little salute with his free hand. Devon watched the precarious pile of books and papers warily. "I'm Winston Egbert."

"Devon. Devon Whitelaw." He extended his hand.

Winston thrust his own hand forward. The mound of objects he was holding began to teeter. Devon caught a notebook in midair and returned it to Winston's arms.

5

"It's OK," Devon said, handing Winston his notebook, "we can shake later."

"Yeah, that's probably a good idea," Winston agreed with a laugh. He shifted the stack of stuff into a more comfortable position.

"You really ought to get a backpack or something," Devon suggested.

"Oh, I have one," Winston returned, nodding enthusiastically. "I spilled grape juice all over it at lunch, so it's hanging in my locker drying out."

Devon suppressed a smile. *It figures,* he thought. *I should have guessed as much.*

"Well, it was nice meeting you," Devon said, backing away. "I gotta go meet with a guidance counselor."

"Oh, so you're starting here soon?" Winston asked.

"Monday," Devon confirmed. "Hey, good luck on your quiz."

Winston stiffened. "Yikes! My quiz!" he exclaimed. "I've got to run! If I'm late for English again, Mr. Collins is going to *kill* me." He dashed down the hall away from Devon. When he had advanced a few paces, he turned around and walked backward for a moment.

"Hey, thanks a lot, Devon," he called back. "It was nice to meet you."

"Watch out!" Devon called nervously as Winston nearly ran into a crowd of students standing just

6

outside one of the classrooms. He heard Winston apologize to the group and excuse himself as he squeezed past them. Devon couldn't help laughing out loud.

If I ever hang out with that guy, I'm going to have to remember to walk behind him, he thought wryly.

Once Winston had disappeared around the corner and Devon was certain the halls were safe again, he continued along the corridor until he came to the main office.

Devon swung open the heavy wooden door and introduced himself to the secretary who was seated directly in front of it. Almost immediately he was shown into one of the guidance counselors' offices. It seemed as if they'd been expecting him. Nan must have called in advance.

Devon was examining the volumes of classic books on the shelves of the office when the guidance counselor walked in briskly.

"Good afternoon, Devon," he said, offering his hand. "My name is Mr. Farrington, and I'd like to welcome you to Sweet Valley High."

Devon quickly rose to greet the counselor and attempted to return the firm handshake with equal strength. Mr. Farrington was an imposing man about six and a half feet tall. He had a stern voice, smooth ebony skin, dark eyes, and chiseled features.

7

But when Mr. Farrington smiled, his whole face lit up. Devon relaxed somewhat.

"I understand you've had quite a journey," Mr. Farrington began. "I'd like to begin by saying that I'm sorry for your recent loss."

"Thank you," Devon responded, a bit startled by the counselor's comments. It was a nice sentiment, but Devon began to wonder just how much Nan had told the school about him. He had hoped to start fresh in Sweet Valley and didn't need people knowing all about his wealthy background and high IQ—and he certainly didn't want anyone's pity.

"I've received your transcripts from Westwood Academy, and I'm quite impressed with your record," Mr. Farrington said candidly. "It seems that you've tested at the genius level in mathematics and the general sciences and earned honors in all your other classes." Mr. Farrington paused to smile at Devon. "That's rather remarkable, you know."

Devon managed a weak smile but was unable to look enthusiastic as the guidance counselor continued to list his accomplishments.

"Science fair winner grades five through ten, math award both freshman and sophomore year, outstanding achievement in biology as well as algebra one and two . . . it goes on and on," Mr.

Farrington said, beaming. Devon merely shrugged.

For years Devon's teachers had patted him on the back, praising his accomplishments and telling him only a student with devoted parents could achieve such things. They continually emphasized how lucky he was, but Devon didn't agree. He gladly would have traded his high IQ and every one of his achievements for a father who played catch with him or a mother who asked him how his day was.

The large man looked Devon in the eyes.

"Let's get down to business, Mr. Whitelaw," he said. "Given the information from your previous school and the information Ms. Johnstone provided over the phone, I've taken the liberty of putting together a schedule for you." He paused and began rifling through the papers on his desk.

Here we go again, Devon thought. *I've already been labeled, and they'll be enrolling me in some gifted and talented program any minute now. So much for anonymity.* He sat back heavily in the black antique captain's chair and slumped down. He watched Mr. Farrington flipping through the forms on the desk and resigned himself to his fate.

It seemed he would always have other people in control of his life. His parents had placed him in special school programs, pushing him to finish at the top of his class and gain recognition. Now it appeared the same thing was going to happen in Sweet Valley.

"Ah, here we are," Mr. Farrington said, looking up again. He handed Devon a sample schedule with space for seven classes plus lunch. To Devon's surprise, only two courses had been penciled in. The rest of the squares on the grid were blank.

"I've enrolled you in AP chemistry and calculus to start out," Mr. Farrington told him. "If you don't find those challenging enough, you let me know right away. We might be able to work out something through our partnership with Sweet Valley University. Some of our students take classes there to bolster their transcripts."

"You mean I'm only taking two classes?" Devon asked, dumbfounded.

Mr. Farrington grinned kindly. "Of course not." He chuckled. "You'll have to fill in the other five blocks yourself. One of them has to be an English class and you'll need one history, but aside from that you're on your own." Devon simply stared. Was this guy for real?

"Well, you didn't think I was going to make all your decisions for you, did you?" the guidance counselor asked.

Devon felt a little foolish for having been so cynical. But after all he had been through, he had trouble trusting people. Before Devon had found

Nan, he had nearly been taken in by two sets of conniving relatives—people who had pretended to care about him but were really interested in his money. He reminded himself of a promise he made to Nan—to try to see the good in people before jumping to conclusions.

"We like to challenge our students, Devon," Mr. Farrington explained. "But we also want you to have a well-rounded education. That means you need to be involved in it. We want you to pursue *your* interests, not ours."

Devon was astonished.

Mr. Farrington reached into his file cabinet and pulled out a brochure. "Here's a list of the electives we offer at Sweet Valley High," he said, offering the booklet to Devon. "Why don't you look through the descriptions, make some choices, and let me know what you decide. Then we can check the computer and see what fits your schedule. How's that sound?"

"Great," Devon replied enthusiastically. He looked up at Mr. Farrington and smiled. *Maybe things will be different here after all,* he thought. *Now all I have to do is find that blond girl, and everything will fall into place.*

Jessica Wakefield was scanning the student parking lot for Lila Fowler's green Triumph convertible

11

when she noticed him. Standing next to a sporty-looking motorcycle was one of the cutest guys she had ever seen, and he was staring right back at her.

His gaze was so intense, Jessica couldn't have looked away if she had wanted to—but she definitely didn't want to. She eyed the stranger carefully, taking in every detail of his appearance. He was easily six feet tall, with a lean, muscular frame. His dark brown hair was cut short on the sides with more length on top, making him appear at once sophisticated and untamed. The cut also accentuated his strong, square jaw. He had full lips, and even from a distance Jessica could see the slate blue color of his eyes. Jessica wondered if he was the new student she had heard her friends talking about earlier. A few people had noticed him in the office that afternoon when he was registering for classes. *He's even hotter than they said*, Jessica thought.

She watched him pull on his helmet, totally unable to take her eyes off him. And he seemed to be having a hard time looking away from her too.

Naturally, Jessica thought. *What man has ever been able to resist me?* But she had to admit that this guy certainly had some charm of his own.

His faded blue jeans and white T-shirt fit perfectly, showing off his strong, athletic build. With his brown leather jacket hanging loosely on his

12

frame, he looked like the ultimate rebel. *Definitely dangerous,* Jessica thought, admiring him. *Especially on that bike.*

Jessica recalled the tragedies her family had suffered because of motorcycles. Her cousin, Rexy, had been killed in a motorcycle accident just three years ago. Then, more recently, her twin sister, Elizabeth, had been in a coma as a result of a similar incident. For a while Jessica had sworn she would never ride on a motorcycle herself, but she had since come to the conclusion that if handled properly, a motorcycle could be as safe as a car. She wasn't about to run out and buy one for herself, but she had been known to accept a ride from a cute guy on a bike from time to time.

And that's one guy I wouldn't mind riding with, she thought. She pictured herself on the back of his bike with her arms wrapped tightly around his waist. The image made her smile. *I could use a little excitement in my life right now,* she thought. Closing her eyes, she imagined how it would feel to cruise down the road with the wind in her face. All eyes would be on her as she and her motorcycle hunk motored through town. Everyone would want to be as cool as she was. *But then,* she thought, *doesn't everybody already want to be like me?*

Suddenly Jessica was startled by the sound of the motorcycle engine getting louder. She realized she had been daydreaming and opened her eyes just in time to see the guy on the motorcycle coming toward her. She stared longingly as the bike got closer. Then, just as he was about to pass her by, he turned and met her gaze.

He's looking right at me, Jessica thought excitedly. Her heart was pounding. *Is this what love at first sight is like?* She stared back and held his gaze for what seemed like an eternity. His stony blue eyes were positively riveted on her. She felt her spine tingle as he got closer.

Talk about intense, she thought. *This is one guy I'm definitely going to get to know. Motorcycle or no motorcycle.*

It's her, Devon thought, his heart pounding as he drove toward the beautiful girl standing outside the school, *and she's staring right back at me.* Devon's cool composure was shattered as he stared at the blond goddess on the high-school lawn.

From her shiny blond hair blowing in the wind to her gorgeous blue-green eyes, she was exactly as he had always pictured the ideal girl to be. She was vibrant and healthy, with a slim, athletic figure. She wore a simple, pale blue tank dress that fluttered in the wind. It had narrow shoulder straps that accentuated her long, elegant arms and graceful neck. The knee-length flared hemline showed off her shapely calves without revealing too much.

But what was even more important to Devon was that he sensed she was someone he could connect with. He had felt it the other night when he had first seen her at the football game. He could tell she was intelligent, and when he had seen her talking with her friend in the stands, she had looked kind and caring as well. Devon stared directly into her eyes as he rode by, and a warm, tingling sensation ran down his back as she returned his gaze. Before he knew it, he was cruising down the road again, the school and the blond girl far behind him. But as he drove away, her image stayed with him.

He imagined riding back to the school and picking her up on his bike.

They would cruise down the highway together, her arms wrapped tightly around his waist and her head nestled against his shoulder. When they arrived at her house, she'd invite him in for dinner. They would hit it off right away, and her parents would love him too. Then they'd stay up half the night watching old movies, eating popcorn, and just talking. Soon they'd be dating and—

Whoa! Slow down, Whitelaw, he cautioned himself. Not only was he getting carried away with his fantasy, but he was actually going fifteen miles per hour over the speed limit. He eased up on the throttle and brought himself back down to a comfortable cruising pace, both on his bike and in his mind.

I'll just have to wait a little longer, he told himself. *On Monday, I'll get my chance to learn everything there is to know about my dream girl.*

Chapter 2

"Hello? Earth to Jessica!"

Startled, Jessica jumped slightly when she heard Lila Fowler's voice.

"Oh, sorry," she replied, still staring down the road where the guy on the bike had gone. Lila followed Jessica's gaze and then looked her in the eyes.

"The beach is west of us, the mall is to our north, and I'm standing just east of you," Lila said sarcastically. "Exactly what are you finding of interest over there?"

Jessica smiled devilishly. "Oh, nothing," she said, tucking her hair behind her ears nonchalantly. "Only the cutest guy to hit Sweet Valley High in decades."

Lila's eyes widened. "You saw the new guy?" she asked excitedly.

"Did I ever," Jessica said, feeling a surge of excitement as she recalled the way his mysterious eyes had locked on hers.

"Well?" Lila prodded, grabbing Jessica's wrist. "Give me the details. What'd he look like? Was he as cute as everyone was saying?"

"Cuter," Jessica answered. "And *très* cool."

"Was he as cute as your brother, Steven?" Lila asked teasingly as they began to walk across the parking lot. "You know, my *fiancé*."

Jessica stopped smiling and scowled at Lila instead.

"That wasn't funny, you know. You really had Liz and me worried," Jessica said seriously. Lila waved a hand in the air dismissively.

"Oh, lighten up. You two deserved it after what you tried to pull," Lila returned.

Over the past month Lila had been dating the twins' older brother, Steven. When Jessica and Elizabeth had found out about it, they were appalled. They had done everything they could think of to break Lila and Steven up, but nothing seemed to work. What the two sisters didn't realize, however, was that the "happy couple" had already decided not to see each other anymore. But when Lila and Steven figured out that the twins had been trying to sabotage their relationship all along, they decided to play their own joke and had convinced the twins that they were engaged to be married.

"Maybe we shouldn't have tried so hard to break you two up," Jessica responded. "But pretending you were engaged was just plain cruel."

"Whatever," Lila said, ignoring Jessica's statement entirely. "Forget about that. Tell me about the new guy."

Jessica was glad to turn the conversation back to the hunk on the bike. She immediately began gushing about the guy's appearance and how he couldn't take his eyes off her. Jessica raved about his muscular body and gorgeous eyes all the way to Lila's car. When she was finished, Lila seemed disappointed.

"He rides a Harley-Davidson?" Lila asked, looking somewhat disgusted.

"I didn't expect you to be impressed by the bike," Jessica said. "But trust me. One look at this guy and even you would be tempted to ride with him."

Lila looked doubtful. "I don't think so, Jess," she answered. "For one thing, Donna Karan gowns don't travel well on the back of motorcycles. And for another, I usually prefer Armani jackets over leather ones." Lila brushed the shoulder of her sleek black jacket, and Jessica rolled her eyes.

Jessica knew that the motorcycle wasn't Lila's

only reason for acting aloof. Clearly Lila was jealous because Jessica had seen the new guy first. In addition to being Jessica's best friend, Lila was also one of her biggest rivals. They were in constant competition over everything from boys to clothing.

"Well, it doesn't matter if you think he's cute or not," Jessica said. "I certainly do, and by the end of next week I intend to be riding on the back of that motorcycle." Jessica shot Lila a determined look and opened the passenger-side door to the Triumph. "Now, weren't we headed to the mall?"

"Absolutely," Lila replied, opening her door and sliding into the sporty convertible. "My post-fire wardrobe leaves a great deal to be desired. Tonight, Ms. Wakefield, you and I are taking Valley Mall by storm!" Lila declared, as though she were leading troops into battle.

Jessica laughed. It was nice to have Lila back. Recently her exquisite mansion had burned down, and for a couple of weeks after the fire Lila had been totally depressed and rather, well, boring. But now that the renovations were done, Lila was back to her old shopaholic self.

"No boutique is safe!" Lila proclaimed, turning the key in the ignition.

"When has any store ever been safe with Lila Fowler and her credit cards on the prowl?" Jessica said with a smirk. Lila gasped exaggeratedly, pretending to be offended.

"Be nice, and I just might help you find something to impress that motorcycle stud of yours," Lila said playfully.

"Now you're talking," Jessica exclaimed, turning up the radio. "To the mall!"

Lila peeled the car out of the parking lot, and Jessica laughed as the wind whipped through her hair.

"I'm positively stuffed," Elizabeth Wakefield said, sitting back heavily in one of the kitchen chairs at the Wakefield house. "I don't think I could move if I wanted to."

She and her longtime boyfriend, Todd Wilkins, had ordered takeout from one of Sweet Valley's most posh restaurants, La Maison. Their meal of tender chicken basted in a red-wine sauce had come complete with escargots, garden salads, and *crème brûlée* for dessert. Now they were seated at the Wakefields' kitchen table, where Elizabeth was enjoying a cup of decaf *latte* while Todd drank hot chocolate with whipped cream.

"Then don't move," Todd replied, leaning over to kiss her. Elizabeth closed her eyes and enjoyed the feeling of Todd's lips pressed to hers. She put her arms lightly around his neck

21

and felt the soft cotton of his white dress shirt.

Since they had ordered such elegant food, Elizabeth and Todd had decided to dress semiformal for their intimate dinner. Todd wore a silk tie and black cashmere pants with his white shirt. Elizabeth's fitted black vest and matching straight skirt complemented his outfit nicely. They looked like a perfect couple.

Elizabeth broke away and rested her chin on Todd's shoulder, hugging him close. There was nothing she loved more than spending romantic evenings alone with him, and tonight was no exception. As Todd settled back into his chair Elizabeth smiled widely.

"You look so happy," he commented, holding her hand in his and massaging it lightly with his thumb.

"I am," Elizabeth said, beaming. "I feel like everything is perfect in the world right now. I just finished a fabulous meal paired with wonderful conversation, and now I'm going to spend a quiet evening alone with the man of my dreams. I almost wish time could stand still right here."

She looked deep into Todd's coffee brown eyes. He was a great guy, and Elizabeth knew she was lucky to have him. She raised his hand to her lips and kissed it lightly. "I can't think of a single thing that could spoil this moment," she added, moving in to kiss him again.

Just then the front door slammed, causing both Elizabeth and Todd to jump. Elizabeth heard Jessica's voice from the foyer.

"I can think of *one* thing," Todd said, sighing. Elizabeth flashed him a disapproving look as she responded to her sister.

"In here, Jess," Elizabeth called, but before the words were fully out of her mouth, Jessica burst into the kitchen, already talking excitedly.

"And he's *so* cute," Jessica was saying. She reached over Elizabeth's shoulder, grabbed the spoon that was still in the dessert dish, and brought it to her lips.

"Mmmm . . . *crème brûlée*," she said, replacing the spoon in the ramekin. Elizabeth watched her sister move quickly around the kitchen, grabbing a glass and opening the refrigerator. Elizabeth started to speak, but Jessica was unstoppable.

"You wouldn't believe it if you had seen him yourself, Liz," Jessica continued, pouring herself a glass of iced tea. "Hi, Todd," she added as an afterthought, taking a gulp of her drink. "And to top it off, I already know that he likes me—"

"Wait a minute," Elizabeth interrupted, holding up a hand like a stop signal. "Who are you talking about?"

"Really, Jess," Todd chimed in. "Slow down. Just listening to you is making me dizzy." Jessica

23

rolled her eyes. She put her hands on her hips and looked at both of them.

"I'm talking about the new guy," she said, sounding impatient.

"What new guy?" Elizabeth asked, completely baffled. Jessica pulled out a chair and sat down.

"It figures you two would be behind on the gossip." Jessica shook her head. "You're such an old married couple." She took another long drink from her glass.

Elizabeth shot an amused look at Todd. Her sister never failed to amaze either of them with her direct manner. Sometimes it was difficult to believe Elizabeth and Jessica were sisters, let alone twins. Although they were physically identical, from their shoulder-length blond hair and sparkling blue-green eyes to their slim, athletic builds, their similarities ended there.

This type of off-the-wall, impulsive attitude was typical of Jessica. She was always diving into things headfirst without considering any of the possible consequences. Elizabeth was more inclined to analyze situations and approach them cautiously and rationally after weighing the options. While Elizabeth was a true thinker, Jessica was a woman of action. And if Jessica ever ended up getting into any trouble—which she inevitably did—she always managed to wriggle free unscathed, often with the help of her more responsible sister. Elizabeth preferred to avoid sticky situations altogether and was therefore often considered to be the more mature twin, even though she was only four minutes older.

Jessica swallowed a mouthful of iced tea and proceeded with her news.

"OK. I'll make this simple for you," she said. "Whether you're aware of it or not, there's a new guy starting school on Monday, and he is absolutely to die for!" Jessica had started out speaking slowly, but her pace was already quickening again.

"I was standing in front of the school waiting for Lila when this new student—aka the sexiest guy in the free world—cruised by me on his motorcycle," she said, looking directly at her sister with a playful smile. "He couldn't take his eyes off me—"

"Who could blame him?" Todd asked sarcastically.

"It was really intense," Jessica announced, ignoring Todd. "I can already tell there's electricity between us." Her eyes shone wildly.

Elizabeth wasn't surprised that her sister had found a new love interest. Jessica wasn't one to go without a boyfriend for long. But she was a bit surprised by her choice.

"Jessica, I can't believe you'd consider getting involved with a guy who owns a motorcycle," she said. "I mean, after what happened to Rexy and then to me . . . you were positively devastated. I thought you'd sworn off motorcycles completely."

Jessica shrugged. "I'm certainly not thinking of trading in the Jeep so I can get a bike myself, but that doesn't mean I'm not going to accept rides from cute guys who happen to own motorcycles," she said.

"Good philosophy, Jess," Todd scoffed, shaking his head. "Never let your personal safety stand in the way of your social life." Jessica exhaled sharply, rolling her eyes again, and Elizabeth laughed under her breath.

"Well, I'm still surprised," Elizabeth resumed. "I mean, you were more affected by my accident than I was. You were the one who kept referring to Todd's bike as a *death machine*."

Jessica dismissed Elizabeth with a wave of her hand. "Oh, maybe, but I'm over that now. Besides," she continued with a mischievous smile, "if you had seen the guy, you'd understand. He's way cooler than any of the other guys at Sweet Valley High." Elizabeth kicked Jessica under the table, which prompted Jessica to pause and look in Todd's direction.

"No offense, Todd," she added halfheartedly.

"None taken," Todd assured her with equal insincerity. Elizabeth looked at Todd apologetically. She knew her sister was sometimes difficult for him to put up with.

26

"Anyway, I'd love to sit here and hang out with you two," Jessica said, rising from her seat. "I'm sure you have exciting plans for the night." Her voice was dripping with sarcasm. "But I have to go over to Lila's. We're going to try on the clothes we bought at the mall today."

"Another trip to the mall, Jess?" Elizabeth asked. "I swear, you might as well live there."

Jessica was unfazed. "A woman must look her best," she countered. "Don't you agree, Todd?" she added flirtatiously. Todd didn't bother to respond.

"Besides, I had to buy a new outfit so I could make a lasting impression on my hunky motorcycle guy at school on Monday," Jessica said as she headed out of the kitchen. "Don't wait up for me," she called back over her shoulder. And with that she was gone. The house was silent, and Elizabeth and Todd were once again left alone.

Todd looked at Elizabeth, obviously reeling from the five minutes with Jessica.

"Who was that anyway?" he joked. Elizabeth laughed and shook her head.

"I don't know," she responded. "But I feel like we just got hit by a tornado."

"She certainly is something else," Todd said with a nod. "I don't think she even noticed she interrupted our quiet dinner."

"Probably not," Elizabeth agreed. "There isn't

much that can distract Jessica when she has a guy on her mind." She paused thoughtfully. "Not even a motorcycle."

Todd looked into Elizabeth's eyes. "Don't tell me you're worried," he said, putting his arm around Elizabeth.

"Maybe just a little," she said with a sigh. "After all, you know the kind of shady characters that ride motorcycles," she joked, taking a stab at Todd. Todd laughed and kissed Elizabeth's chin.

"Yeah, we're a dangerous bunch," he responded in a husky voice. Elizabeth cocked her head and smirked at him.

"But to tell you the truth, I'm more concerned for the guy," Todd said. "He has no idea what's about to hit him."

"It's true," Elizabeth acknowledged lightheartedly. "That poor guy doesn't stand a chance against her. After all, what Jessica wants, Jessica gets."

Chapter 3

Devon arrived at school twenty minutes early on Monday morning. He wanted to make sure he had enough time to find his locker and figure out how to get to his first class. The hallways were already crowded with students hanging out and talking about their weekends. As Devon navigated his way through the throng of people to the junior corridor, he watched the numbers on the gray lockers to his right. Finally he located number 268A. It was a top locker, which he took as a good sign. At least he wouldn't have to crouch on the floor every time he needed a book.

Devon pulled the folded piece of paper that the guidance counselor had given him from the back pocket of his faded blue jeans and found his combination.

"Two turns right to four, one turn left to thirteen, right to seventy," Devon mumbled to himself as he turned the dial. "And then left until it opens." He pulled on the lock and it snapped open easily. Suddenly he was startled by a familiar voice behind him.

"You probably don't want to recite the combination out loud when you do that," the voice said. Devon turned around to see Winston, who smiled at him and extended his arm.

"My hands are free now," Winston said, grinning as Devon clasped his hand. Then he swung a green bag down from his shoulder and held it out, running his hand over the front of it like a spokesperson. "My backpack," he said proudly.

"Not bad," Devon said, admiring Winston's prized possession. "And I don't even see any grape juice stains."

"My mom washed it over the weekend." Winston beamed.

"It's a good thing," Devon jested. "Because I actually have to attend classes today, I won't have time to walk around behind you picking up all the things you drop." Winston laughed, and Devon was glad to see that he could take a joke.

"So is this your locker?" Winston inquired, pointing to the empty compartment in front of

Devon. Devon held out the form he had received from Mr. Farrington.

"According to my little piece of paper, it is," he answered. "Anywhere near yours?"

"Pretty close, actually," Winston replied as he began to work on the combination to the locker right next to Devon's.

"Do you mean to tell me I'm going to have to put up with seeing you every morning and afternoon for the rest of the school year?" Devon asked with mock horror. Winston smirked back at him.

"I guess so," he answered, continuing to fidget with his lock. "Unless, of course, you want to work out some kind of schedule so we can avoid being here at the same time."

"That's OK," Devon responded, after pretending to think it over. "At least this way I'll know where you are, and I won't have to worry about getting bowled over from out of nowhere. That's a serious advantage."

Winston laughed as he opened his locker door, then proceeded to drop a few things on the floor.

Devon shook his head and started to get ready himself, removing his jacket and hanging it on the metal hook in his locker. Next he opened his book bag, which was a leather satchel that attached to the side of his bike. He removed a thin notebook and a pencil and then put the bag in his locker. He tucked the pencil behind his ear automatically.

Aside from his scientific calculator, which he knew he'd be needing for calculus, Devon hadn't bothered to buy any school supplies yet. He figured he'd have a better idea of what to get after his first day of classes, and he could easily make a quick trip to the department store on his way home after school.

Devon glanced inside his locker one more time and then slammed the door. As he did so, Winston closed his locker too and turned to face him.

"Hey, thanks again for helping me out the other day. I would've gotten trampled without you there," Winston said.

"It was no problem, really," he assured Winston.

"Well, I owe you one anyway," Winston said with a smile.

"Hold that thought," Devon said, holding up one finger. He took another folded paper from his back pocket. "You might be able to pay me back right now." He examined the slip in his hand, which contained his course schedule.

"I don't suppose you know where Mr. Russo's room is, do you?" he asked, looking up at Winston. "I have him for chemistry first period."

"Oh, sure," Winston responded eagerly. "You just head down the hall and take a right. Russo's room is the first door on the left."

Devon followed Winston's gestures with his eyes. "Thanks. Now we're even," he said, glancing down at his watch. "I've got to get going. I don't want to be late on my first day. Catch you later." He nodded a quick good-bye and turned to leave.

"Whether you want to or not, neighbor," Winston shot back, pointing at their lockers. Devon chuckled and headed off to his class.

He followed Winston's directions, and sure enough, there was Mr. Russo's room. Most of the students were either at their desks or standing just outside the door while they waited for the bell. Devon made his way into the classroom and looked around.

The back of the class consisted of several large lab tables. Each one had two stools per side and two large steel sinks in the middle. In addition, the far wall of the room was lined with shelves containing scales, boxes of rubber gloves, safety goggles, and various other lab supplies. A locked door in the very back was marked with a skull and crossbones and a sign that read Danger: Hazardous Materials. Devon knew that the numerous chemicals used for lab experiments must be locked in that closet. The front half of the classroom contained rows of desks, which faced a large blackboard. There was also another lab table where the teacher could demonstrate experiments to the

33

class. Standing next to the table was an older man, who Devon guessed must be Mr. Russo.

As the teacher moved aside, Devon's heart nearly stopped. Standing right there was the beautiful blonde. Devon had been hoping to meet her, but he hadn't expected her to be in his first class. Mr. Russo turned and noticed Devon.

"Mr. Whitelaw?" the teacher inquired. When Devon nodded, Mr. Russo gestured for him to come to the front of the room. Devon wove his way through the cluttered rows of desks. He couldn't take his eyes off his dream girl. By the time he reached the front of the room, his heart was pounding.

"I'm Mr. Russo, Devon," the older man said, offering his hand, "and this is Elizabeth Wakefield."

The blond girl extended her arm as well. "Hi," she said. "It's nice to meet you."

Devon grasped her hand, looking her straight in the eye. "Elizabeth?" he inquired. He wanted to be certain he had her name right. She nodded casually, smiling at him. It was, without a doubt, the most beautiful smile Devon had ever seen.

As he shook her hand his heart pounded furiously. He felt a warm sensation shoot up his arm and spread throughout his body. Elizabeth's eyes widened slightly, and he was sure she had felt it too. He was trying hard to play it cool and avoid appearing overanxious, but it was difficult. As Elizabeth started to loosen her grip Devon realized he didn't want to let go. Reluctantly he allowed her hand to drop, remaining in contact with her until the last possible second.

"So, Devon," Elizabeth said. "It looks like we're going to be lab partners."

"Really?" Devon said quickly. He grimaced when he heard the gleeful squeak in his voice. *Cool it, Whitelaw,* he chided himself. *You don't want to scare her away.*

"Yes, really," Elizabeth said with a short giggle. The sound of her laughter sent a tingle down his spine. Devon had never had this kind of reaction to a girl before.

Mr. Russo started to give Devon an overview of the class, but Devon wasn't paying attention. As Elizabeth turned to talk to a friend Devon studied her carefully. In a matter of seconds he came to the conclusion that everything about his dream girl was indeed perfect.

She had a kind, warm smile, and he felt as if he could stare into her beautiful eyes forever. Even her style of clothing was perfect. She wore a simple short-sleeve light blue sweater with a V neck and pearl buttons down the front. Together with her crisp white linen pants and white leather sandals it was a perfect ensemble.

Devon preferred clothing that was somewhat on the conservative side. He was more interested in people than in what they wore and hated to see a girl drowned out by her wardrobe. He had never been a fan of girls who dressed in outfits that were too flashy or revealing.

"So, Elizabeth," Mr. Russo said when he finished describing the latest lab experiment to Devon. "Why don't you show Devon to his seat? He can take the empty desk next to yours, and then you can get started on the lab."

"Sure!" Elizabeth answered. "We might as well just throw him right into the insanity."

All right, Devon silently cheered. Not only would she be his lab partner, but he'd get to sit next to her during lecture classes too. *And I thought I was doing well when I got a top locker.*

Devon struggled to remain calm but found it hard to contain his excitement. Not only was he finally meeting the girl of his dreams, but he was guaranteed plenty of time to get to know her. He looked over at Elizabeth again and noticed her gorgeous eyes staring back at him.

He'd only been in school for twenty-five minutes, and already things were definitely off to a great start.

Elizabeth made her way back to the lab tables and took a seat next to the new guy—Devon

Whitelaw. It seemed natural that Mr. Russo had asked her to be Devon's lab partner. She was considered to be one of the top students in the class, and this wasn't the first time she had been paired with a new student to help guide him through a first class.

The odd thing had been the intense shock she had gotten when his hand had touched hers. That feeling of tingly excitement was something Elizabeth hadn't felt in a long time. She struggled to brush it off as she took her seat at the lab table.

Since Devon was new, Elizabeth decided she should probably just take charge and get things started. Getting right to work would also help take her mind off the instant connection she had felt with him.

"Our lab assignment is to test the acid and base levels of various liquids," she said, looking at Devon. He simply stared back at her and nodded silently.

He probably just wants me to lead him through the process, she thought. She reached back to one of the shelves behind them and grabbed a few test tubes and beakers, which she set on their table. Devon took one and fiddled with it while Elizabeth continued speaking.

"I thought we could begin by determining if vinegar is an acid or a base and then work from there," she said, gathering materials as she spoke. She paused to read a little further through her lab notebook and then walked to another shelf and came back with more supplies.

"OK," she continued, too wrapped up in trying to be a good teacher to notice what Devon was doing. "This is litmus paper," she said, holding out the thin strip in her hand. "It says here that if we put a drop of vinegar on the paper, we can determine if it's an acid or a base." She read slowly to make sure she didn't confuse Devon. When she thought she had given him enough time to digest what she had already said, she continued.

"If it's an acid, the paper will turn dark pink, and if it's a base, the paper will remain blue." Elizabeth pushed her hair behind her ear with one hand. She could just barely see Devon out of the corner of her eye. He was fussing with something hurriedly, and Elizabeth sensed that he didn't want her to see him.

He must have spilled something already, she thought. She resisted looking up at him because she didn't want to make him uncomfortable. *He must be nervous,* she told herself. *It's his first day in a new school, and chemistry probably isn't his strong point. I'll just keep concentrating on explaining this clearly and pretend I don't notice his fidgeting.*

"Now," she continued slowly, noticing that Devon seemed to have relaxed a bit. "If we determine it's an acid, then we can figure out its exact level of acidity by adding it to . . ." Elizabeth looked up, searching for the beaker full of liquid that Mr. Russo had provided them with. All at once she realized what Devon had been up to. She was amazed by what she saw.

In front of her were eight test tubes neatly lined up in their holders. The liquid in the various tubes ranged from a dark red to a light orange-pink, and they had been organized from darkest to lightest, left to right.

He had already gone ahead and tested all the solutions and completed the experiment. Elizabeth's jaw dropped open. She scanned the vials from left to right and back again, and then she looked up at Devon. He sat silently with a half smirk on his face.

"I guess you already understand this stuff, huh?" she finally managed, her face reddening. Devon laughed quietly, and a huge smile lit up his face. Elizabeth felt foolish for having gone into such great detail about the lab. Clearly Devon knew more about chemistry than she had anticipated.

"I must have sounded ridiculous," she said, placing both hands on her forehead and looking up at Devon, embarrassed. Suddenly he looked concerned.

"Not at all," he answered quickly. "And I didn't mean to make you feel foolish. I just wanted to surprise you."

Elizabeth saw that he was sincere, and she felt somewhat better.

"Well, you certainly did that," she replied with a small smile. "I thought I was supposed to be helping you out, but obviously you know a lot more about this stuff than I do."

"We just covered it in my old school," he explained modestly. A wide grin lit Devon's face, and his slate blue eyes sparkled. Elizabeth's heart fluttered. This guy was totally gorgeous.

As she stared at him she remembered Jessica's insinuation that if she had seen the new guy, she wouldn't care about the motorcycle. Elizabeth now understood what Jessica meant. The longer Elizabeth looked at him, the more difficult she found it to look away. Suddenly she became aware that she had been holding his gaze for an inappropriately long time. She cleared her throat.

"Well," she said, looking down at her notebook, "since we—I mean *you*—finished the experiment already, I guess we should probably start writing up the lab report." She fidgeted with her pen and tried to look casual.

40

"We've got plenty of time for that," Devon answered, leaning forward. "So tell me," he said, smiling his gorgeous smile. "What's your favorite color?"

"Blue," she told him, tilting her head suspiciously. "Why do you ask?"

"What shade of blue?" Devon asked, ignoring her question. "Light blue, navy blue, royal blue . . ."

"No . . . deep blue, like the ocean on a cold day," Elizabeth said.

"Ahh," Devon sighed. "You mean like the sky at night, just before the sun has completely set, when there's still just a trace of light on the horizon?" he asked.

Wow, Elizabeth thought. *I guess chemistry isn't the only thing he's good at. He sounds like a poet too.* Once again she felt that she might have been staring at him for too long.

"Exactly," she said, feigning a quick cough and looking away. "But I still don't see why . . ." Her voice trailed off as she watched Devon. He began mixing the various liquids on the table together in one of the empty beakers. He worked quietly and quickly, completely focused on what he was doing. Then, with a flourish of his hand, he presented the beaker to Elizabeth. It was filled with liquid of exactly the color blue that she had described.

"That's incredible," she said, amazed. "Now just

get me some sand, and we'll be in business," she joked. She was about to ask him how he had known which liquids to mix, but before she could, he was busily working again.

"You know," he said, pouring liquid from tube to tube as he spoke, "this is really close to your eye color, but it needs a bit more green." Elizabeth watched closely as Devon continued combining the contents, and soon enough he was presenting the beaker to her again.

"It's a pretty good match," Devon said, holding the vial next to her cheek. "But I guess there's just no duplicating the original." He stared into her eyes as he spoke, and Elizabeth couldn't help but stare back. She was flattered that he had noticed her eyes and even more flattered by his comment.

"What about your eyes?" she asked, trying to make a game of Devon's mixing. "Can you match your own color?"

Devon laughed. "Why would I want to do something like that?" he asked. "Wouldn't I be a bit vain if I went around mixing up my own eye color all the time?"

Elizabeth laughed with him. "Well, the least you could do is explain to me how you're doing all of this," she said. "I am your lab partner, you know. You shouldn't keep secrets of this magnitude from me."

"You've got me there," Devon said, smiling. He

showed Elizabeth how to mix various colors, explaining that the greater the acidity of a liquid, the darker red it would turn the purple-colored litmus solution. In addition, anything that was a base would turn the liquid blue.

"The vinegar has a yellowish color," Devon explained. "When you combine the litmus with vinegar, you get red. And some of the litmus solution combined with a base gives you blue. So here I have the three primary colors—yellow, red, and blue. Then, by mixing them in various proportions to one another, I can make any color I want."

Devon created the three colors in separate vials and then began mixing them in the smaller test tubes. Elizabeth listened closely as Devon explained what he was doing every step of the way. His descriptions were incredibly clear, and he demonstrated everything as he talked about it so that she could see how it worked. She was positively amazed. In fifteen minutes with Devon she felt that she had learned more than she ever could from Mr. Russo.

This is fantastic, Elizabeth thought. *He's so smart, and he really knows what he's doing. I'm definitely going to enjoy being his lab partner.* And though she didn't want to admit it to herself, Elizabeth knew that Devon's good looks certainly wouldn't hurt either.

❧　　❧　　❧

Jessica walked across the quad in the center of Sweet Valley High at lunchtime. She was headed for the picnic table where Lila, Amy Sutton, and a few of her other friends from the cheerleading squad had gathered. Jessica was just lamenting the fact that she hadn't yet seen her hunky motorcycle guy when she spotted him.

Her heart caught in her throat. He was standing alone in the shade of one of the tall palm trees that dotted the high-school campus, the leaves throwing a mysterious shadow across his clean-cut features. This guy was perfection personified. Jessica straightened the skirt of her white minidress and pressed her lips together. It was time to meet the new love of her life.

Prepare to be charmed, biker boy, she said to herself as she approached him.

As she got closer she was surprised to see him glance up and smile. He seemed to be looking at her as though he already knew her.

Wow, I guess I didn't imagine the electricity between us the other day, she thought. *He obviously remembers me.* She put on her most vibrant Jessica Wakefield smile and got ready to greet him, but to her surprise he spoke first.

"Hey, how about that chemistry?" he said, his beautiful blue eyes sparkling. Jessica was puzzled by his comment at first. But in a warm rush she realized he must be referring to the moment of intense eye contact they had shared when he left the school on Friday.

So he felt it too, she thought, blown away by his direct approach. But just as she was about to answer him, she noticed that he was distracted by something behind her. She turned to see Elizabeth, accompanied by her two best friends, Enid Rollins and Maria Slater, walking toward the picnic tables. Jessica turned back to her motorcycle guy, who was looking from her to Elizabeth and back again. He appeared to be totally confused. Jessica realized what was going on and laughed.

"That's my twin sister, Elizabeth," she explained. "I'm Jessica—the better half of a matched pair," she added flirtatiously, extending her hand to him.

"I'm Devon," he said distractedly.

Devon. What a sexy name, Jessica thought with a smile. But instead of shaking her hand, Devon was looking over her shoulder again.

Jessica turned to follow his gaze, and this time she noticed that Elizabeth was looking in her direction and waving. She was about to wave back, but then she realized Elizabeth was actually looking just past her, to Devon. Jessica turned to face him and was surprised to see him waving back. Now it was her turn to be confused.

"Have you already met Liz?" she asked.

"Yeah. She was in my chem class this morning," Devon answered, still watching as Elizabeth made her way to the picnic tables. "You know, 'how about that chemistry?'" he said, glancing at Jessica almost as if it was an afterthought. "I thought you were her."

Jessica was embarrassed when she realized she had misunderstood his comment. An uncharacteristic blush rose to her cheeks, but her feelings of awkwardness didn't last long. *Big deal,* she told herself. *So he met Liz in chemistry first. He's still cute, and he's still new, and he's still going to need someone to show him around. And who better than the ever charming Jessica Wakefield?* She perked up again, already forgetting her temporary unease.

"So," she began, flipping her hair over her shoulder, "you're lucky you met me."

"Why's that?" Devon asked, finally focusing all his attention on her.

"Because I am the most fabulous tour guide at Sweet Valley High," Jessica said enthusiastically. "I can show you the coolest hangouts, the best restaurants, the hippest dance clubs. Plus I can introduce you to all the right people," she added, certain he would jump at the chance to hang out with the most popular, not to mention gorgeous, girl in school.

"OK, sure . . . sometime," he said shifting his weight from one leg to the other. "Nice to meet you, Jessica." He smiled briefly, then turned and walked away.

At first Jessica was stunned by his brush-off, but as she watched him saunter off, her heart fluttered again.

"Playing it cool, are we, biker boy?" she murmured with a sly grin. "I can handle cool."

Devon was definitely intriguing. In his beat-up jeans and leather jacket, he was a refreshing change from the boring sappy boys at Sweet Valley High. He was mysterious. And with mystery came danger. Jessica was totally determined to make him hers.

She turned and began walking over to join her friends. *Wait until I tell Lila and Amy that I talked to the new guy*, Jessica thought. *They'll be so jealous.* She quickened her pace, eager to share her news. On her way to the table she pictured herself riding on the back of Devon's motorcycle, wearing his leather jacket and clutching him around the waist as they roared along the beach together.

She couldn't wait until it happened, and she had no doubt that it would. Soon. After all, however cool, Devon was still a guy, and Jessica Wakefield knew how to get to guys. She vowed to herself that Devon would be no exception.

Chapter 4

"So how was the first day?" Nan asked as she took a few vegetables from the refrigerator and handed them to Devon.

"It was pretty good," Devon answered, weighing the question in his mind. "In fact, as far as first days go, I'd have to say it was great," he said, tossing a tomato into the air and catching it behind his back with his other hand. Nan smiled at his antics.

"Well, you're certainly in a good mood," she said. "Anything you feel like talking about?"

Devon knew Nan was eager to be involved in his life. It was clear she hoped to reestablish the close relationship they had shared when he was a young boy and she was his nanny. Some people might be put off by her tendency to ask personal questions, but Devon didn't mind at all. He knew he could trust Nan, and it had been a long time since there had been anyone in his life he could really talk to. He was glad to finally have an adult around who genuinely cared about him.

"Well," he began slowly, glancing at Nan out of the corner of his eye. She leaned closer to him with obvious interest. Devon could tell she was dying to hear the details of his day, but he was having fun teasing her. "There was this one girl. . . ." He let his voice trail off and observed Nan's reaction.

She continued rolling the chicken in flour and bread crumbs, but she kept doing the same piece over and over again even though it was already coated.

"Out with it already!" she exclaimed, smiling at him. "You can't just leave me hanging like that." Devon laughed. He enjoyed having Nan in his life again. *I really missed her over the years,* he thought. *It's nice to be home.* Finally he let Nan off the hook.

"OK," he said, "I did meet a girl that I'm kind of excited about. Her name is Elizabeth Wakefield, and she's in my chemistry class, and she's positively beautiful, and intelligent, and sweet, and funny, and witty—" Devon stopped himself. He could have continued forever, but he realized he was beginning to ramble.

"Wow," Nan responded. "It sounds like she

49

made quite an impression on you. Did you determine all of this in one class period?"

"It was a *double* period," Devon corrected her, grinning. He quickly sliced up a carrot, then grabbed a cucumber. "Chemistry *and* chem lab. And I could tell she was special the moment I saw her."

"She certainly sounds like one of a kind," Nan said, finally placing the chicken breast into a pan and starting on a fresh one. Devon couldn't help laughing at her comment.

"Actually she's not," he said. He slid the sliced vegetables off the cutting board and into the large wooden salad bowl. Nan gave him a puzzled look. "I found out at lunch that she has an identical twin sister," he explained.

"Ohhh," Nan murmured, raising one eyebrow. "That could create problems. Two beautiful girls who look exactly alike. How could you decide which one to date?"

"That's the funny thing," Devon responded. "They're both gorgeous, and I'm not sure I could tell them apart just by looking at them, but they're not at all alike."

"What do you mean?" Nan asked, putting the chicken in the oven and setting the timer. Devon tossed the salad with a pair of tongs and splashed some vinaigrette over the top. When he was done, he turned to face Nan and folded his arms across his chest.

"When I met Elizabeth, something seemed to click right away," he said thoughtfully. "She's really down-to-earth and easy to talk to."

"Sounds like a nice girl," Nan said.

"She is," Devon said, remembering how welcoming and kind Elizabeth had been. "She was assigned to be my lab partner today, and even though I already knew how to do a lot of the stuff we were studying, she didn't get all quiet and just let me do the work. And by the end of the period I think she had a better grasp of it than I did. She really is amazing."

"And what about her sister?" Nan asked, grabbing a sponge to wipe some stray bread crumbs off the counter and into the garbage can.

"Jessica . . . ," Devon said, knitting his brow as he considered Elizabeth's twin. "Well, I'll say this for her—she's certainly full of energy."

"That's not a bad thing," Nan said. She replaced the garbage can under the sink and rinsed her hands. Devon took a towel from the rack and leaned forward to hand it to her.

"No," Devon said, narrowing his eyes in thought. "But she's just not my type." He laughed out loud. "It seems weird since she and Elizabeth are identical, but I'm really drawn to Elizabeth, and I don't think I'm the least bit interested in Jessica. She was nice and everything, but when I talked to her, all she wanted to do was show me all the hippest places in town and introduce me to all the *right* people. Not exactly the kind of stuff that interests me."

"Well, you've only known her for one day," Nan said thoughtfully. "There may be more to her than meets the eye."

"I'm sure there is," Devon replied. "But something about Jessica just doesn't appeal to me."

"But something about Elizabeth does," Nan said.

"Yeah. Elizabeth just seems . . ." He hesitated, searching for the right word. "*Deeper* than Jessica." He looked at Nan to see if any of what he was saying was making sense to her.

"It sounds like you've really thought this through," she said, "and from what you've told me, I'd say Elizabeth sounds more like the girl for you too." Devon was glad to hear that Nan shared his opinion.

"You always were a highly intelligent child," she said. "If you've found someone who can match your intellect, I'd say you're doing well."

"Trust me, she can," he assured Nan, grinning.

"She sounds wonderful," Nan said.

Devon laughed. It was nice to know that Nan

believed in him and trusted his judgment.

Being trusted wasn't something Devon was used to. His parents had never wanted him to date anyone until they could be sure she belonged to an appropriate country club and had parents who were from the proper social class. That was something Devon had always hated about his parents. They were snobs.

Nan was completely different. Because she had faith in his judgments, she allowed him to make his own decisions. Devon appreciated it, but he knew it would take some getting used to.

"Thanks," he said, looking at Nan sincerely.

"For what?" she asked, a puzzled look crossing her kind face.

"For trusting me," Devon answered. Nan gave him a tender look.

"It's easy," she told him. "But just because I trust you doesn't mean I never want you to introduce me to this girl. When you get to know her better, I definitely want to meet her," she said, shaking her finger at him jocularly. She placed a pot on the stove top and began preparing rice to go with their dinner.

"You got it," Devon answered. He picked up the wooden bowl, carried it out to the dining room, and then returned to the kitchen for plates and silverware so he could set the table.

While he was getting things together, he thought back to chemistry class again. He couldn't help but smile at the memory of Elizabeth's inquisitive smiles and her open attitude. She was so vibrant and beautiful.

Yes, I intend to get to know Elizabeth Wakefield much better, he told himself. *She's definitely something special.*

"She's just so important to me," Todd Wilkins told his parents as he took his last bite of stuffing. "I want to make sure I do something special to celebrate with her."

Todd was eating dinner with his parents in the Wilkinses' kitchen. The cook had the night off, and his mother had prepared a roast chicken with all the fixings. Unlike many of his friends, Todd actually enjoyed hanging out with his parents from time to time. His father was often busy with his company, Varitronics, and his mother had a flourishing catering business, so family dinners were rare. But when they were able to eat together, they usually had a good time.

Todd had just finished explaining to them that next Monday would mark exactly one year since Elizabeth's first article had been published in the *Oracle,* Sweet Valley High's student newspaper. He wanted to do something unique to help celebrate the occasion, but he was having a hard time coming up with ideas.

"How about taking her to dinner?" his father offered.

"Or better yet, make her dinner yourself," his mother chimed in. "A woman likes a man who can cook."

Todd considered his mom's idea. Preparing a home-cooked meal for Elizabeth . . . well, it would definitely surprise her—especially if it came out well.

"You might have something there, Mom," Todd said, resting his chin on his hand. "But there's one problem—I can't cook." Todd's father rose from the table and began to clear away the dishes. "Personally, I think you should go with flowers and candy, son. It worked on your mother."

"When will you learn, Bert?" Mrs. Wilkins teased. "I didn't marry you for the flowers or the candy. I married you for your money."

The two of them laughed. It was true that Bert Wilkins was quite wealthy now, having been promoted to president at Varitronics. But when Todd's parents had first met, Mr. Wilkins had been broke. Todd interrupted his parents' merriment.

"Come on, guys," he pleaded. "Writing is really important to Elizabeth," he explained. "I know she's going to be a famous novelist or journalist someday, so this is a really special occasion. I want to do something different to show her it means as much to me as it does to her." He looked to his parents for advice, but they appeared stumped. Todd's father returned to the table.

"Dinner and flowers are so . . . traditional. I want to do something distinctive," Todd explained.

His parents looked at each other, obviously searching for more ideas, but neither one of them seemed to come up with anything. Finally his mother spoke.

"I guess you're just stuck with traditional parents, Todd. I can't think of a thing." She looked to her husband.

"Neither can I," Mr. Wilkins added. Todd sighed and slumped down a bit in his chair.

"Well, thanks for trying," he said, disappointed. "I guess I'll just go try to get some homework done. I'll figure this out later." He grabbed his backpack as he walked through the foyer and headed up the large staircase that led to the second floor of the Wilkinses' mansion.

As he ascended the stairs Todd started to mull over the idea of cooking for Elizabeth. *I just might give it a try,* he thought. *How hard could it be? And while flowers and candy are kind of traditional, I should probably get her something she'd really want. . . .*

Todd pushed open his bedroom door and walked across the hardwood floor, taking a seat at his large mahogany desk. He fished a pencil from his backpack and pulled out his algebra two book, turning to that night's assignment.

Instead of beginning, though, Todd tapped his pencil on the open book and looked out the large bay window into the Wilkinses' backyard. He stared at the lights that lined the pathway around their rectangular swimming pool and brainstormed some more.

Jewelry, he suddenly thought. *Elizabeth was just saying the other night that aside from her gold lavaliere, she didn't think she had one nice piece of jewelry that she could wear on formal occasions.*

Maybe he could even get Jessica to help him. She knew Elizabeth's tastes better than anyone. *I bet I could get her to help me with the surprise element too,* he told himself. *After all, she is a great schemer.*

Satisfied that he had made some progress in his plans, Todd opened his notebook and began to work on his math problems. He made a mental note to talk to Jessica about the celebration for Elizabeth as soon as he got a chance.

The big event was still a week away, but already Todd was starting to get excited about it. Elizabeth was the love of his life, and he was looking forward to doing something special for her. After all they'd been through together, she deserved it.

Elizabeth sat at the computer in her immaculate room. She was trying to finish typing up her lab report for chemistry class, but she had only gotten as far as the hypothesis. Every time she started writing about the lab, she was inevitably reminded of Devon.

Elizabeth recalled his beautiful slate blue eyes, his magnetic grin, and his unbelievable charm.

And he's so intelligent, she thought. *I still can't believe how much I learned from him in just one class period.*

Looking back to her nearly empty computer screen, Elizabeth straightened up and tried to concentrate.

"You already have a wonderful boyfriend," she told herself, poising her fingers over the keyboard. "If you're going to sit here gushing over anyone, it should be Todd."

She took a deep breath and exhaled sharply to help clear her head. Once she had typed her name and the date in the top-right corner of the page, she tried to think of a good first sentence—but it was no use. She couldn't get Devon's image out of her mind.

She glanced at her watch. *Jessica should be*

home from cheerleading by now, she thought. Elizabeth was dying to pump her sister for details about her meeting with Devon that day at lunch. Elizabeth had been checking her watch every five minutes for the last half hour. Just as she was about to give up on chemistry and try changing subjects, she heard the rustle of pom-poms in the hallway. *Finally,* she thought.

She started to push her chair away from her desk so she could go to Jessica's room, but before Elizabeth could move, Jessica burst through the door. She was wearing bright pink hip-hugging shorts and a black spandex halter top. Obviously she had come straight from practice without changing.

Her outfit showed off her thin waistline and strong stomach muscles. Elizabeth admired the healthy glow of her twin's face. Jessica always looked rejuvenated after a good workout. She bounced into the room and flopped down on Elizabeth's bed, allowing her pom-poms to drop to the floor in front of her.

"You know the guy I was talking to at lunch?" Jessica inquired, not bothering to say hello. Her eyes sparkled with excitement. "The one you waved to?"

"You mean Devon?" Elizabeth asked, trying not to sound too interested. "The guy from my chemistry class?"

"That's the one," Jessica said, smiling. "I thought you might be interested to know that he is indeed my hunky bike guy, and there is definitely electricity between us." Jessica rolled over onto her back and hung her head over the end of Elizabeth's bed, flashing a huge smile.

Elizabeth tried to tell herself she was glad to see her sister so ecstatic but was filled with a strange feeling instead. Jealousy? No, that wasn't possible.

Why would I be jealous? she thought. *Sure, Devon is gorgeous, and witty, and intelligent . . . but that makes him perfect for, well—Jessica,* she told herself forcefully. *And besides, I'm totally in love with Todd. What do I have to be jealous about?*

"Are you listening, Liz?" she heard Jessica's voice call from the bed. Jessica was lying on her stomach again and staring at Elizabeth. "I know your homework is enthralling," she chided. "But try to pay attention. I'm attempting to tell you about my incredible new boyfriend."

"Your *boyfriend?*" Elizabeth exclaimed, unable to believe her ears.

"Well, not officially," Jessica admitted, "but soon enough." Elizabeth felt strangely relieved. She realized that Jessica was just speaking with her usual penchant for embellishment. Of course

60

Devon wasn't her boyfriend yet—she had just met him. That was just Jessica's way of stating that she was officially interested in someone. Elizabeth relaxed.

"Anyway," Jessica continued, "I saw him getting on his bike after school when I was on my way to cheerleading practice. He couldn't stop staring at me. Liz, I think I'm in love!"

"That's great," Elizabeth said with false enthusiasm.

"Did you get much of a chance to talk to him in chemistry class?" Jessica asked. Elizabeth glanced back at her computer screen and thought about the wonderful moments she and Devon had shared. She wanted to tell Jessica about how he mixed her favorite color and then her eye color but decided instead to play it down. She didn't want Jessica to think she was interested in Devon.

"No, not really," she lied. "We had a lot of work to get done. There wasn't much time to talk." Jessica looked disappointed. She had obviously been hoping for some inside information.

"Well," Jessica began, hopping up and sitting with her legs dangling off the side of Elizabeth's bed, her hands supporting her at her sides, "I'm sure *I'll* have plenty of info to share with *you* about the mysterious motorcycle man soon enough. I'm going to be acting as his personal tour guide in Sweet Valley," she stated proudly.

Elizabeth watched as her sister jumped off the bed and grabbed her pom-poms.

"And Devon is just as excited about it as I am," Jessica added, bounding toward the door. "Now, if you'll excuse me, I have to go comb my closet for something positively breathtaking to wear tomorrow." She shot Elizabeth a playful glance. "You know, just in case he asks me to show him around after school."

With that Jessica pranced out of the room. Elizabeth couldn't help but laugh as her sister exited.

"Watch out, Devon," she said quietly. "You're about to be hit by the most devastating force in all of nature—my sister."

Chapter 5

"So what's he like?" Maria Slater asked as she and Elizabeth wove through the corridor on Tuesday morning.

"Who?" Elizabeth returned, sidestepping a couple of freshmen guys who were wrestling on the floor.

"The new guy," Maria prodded. "I heard he's in your chem class."

"Not you too!" Elizabeth exclaimed. Why was everyone so interested in Devon? "News sure travels fast around here."

"Well, I heard he's hot," Maria said, running a hand over her short black curls. "And you seem overly excited to get to first period."

Elizabeth realized she *was* walking rather quickly, but she wasn't about to admit that to Maria.

"I'm not rushing," she said. Suddenly her foot struck something hard and she flew forward, losing her balance completely. A strong arm shot out and caught her before she hit the ground.

"Walk much, Wakefield?" Elizabeth looked up to find the person who had saved her from becoming intimate with the floor was none other than Bruce Patman.

"Always the gentleman, Bruce," Maria snapped sarcastically. Elizabeth straightened her skirt and continued down the hallway.

"Girl, you are totally flustered," Maria said. "What gives?"

"OK," Elizabeth began, stopping to lean against a wall and catch her breath. "He is very good-looking. And maybe I am a little eager to see him. But there's nothing wrong with that."

Maria raised her perfectly plucked eyebrows doubtfully.

"It's only because he's such a nice guy, and I think he could be a good friend," Elizabeth explained desperately.

"You're blushing!" Maria exclaimed.

Elizabeth groaned. "I am not!" she protested, feeling the telltale warmth in her cheeks. "I am perfectly happy with Todd. And besides, Jessica likes Devon." She pushed herself away from the wall and started walking again.

"The poor boy," Maria deadpanned, keeping pace with Elizabeth.

"It'll be nice if Jessica starts seeing him," Elizabeth said, ignoring Maria's comment. She stopped outside Mr. Russo's room and looked her friend in the eye. "She'll finally have a boyfriend I actually like." At this point Elizabeth had almost convinced herself.

"Hey, Liz!" Devon walked by on his way into the classroom, flashing her his heart-stopping grin. Maria's jaw dropped open.

"Was that him?" she hissed. For some reason Elizabeth couldn't find her voice. She just nodded.

"Transfer me to chemistry," Maria said, peeking into the room. She turned back around and looked at Elizabeth with an almost sympathetic expression. "Good luck," she said. She patted Elizabeth's arm before walking away.

I'm gonna need it, Elizabeth thought, taking a few deep breaths in an attempt to calm her racing heart. *All I want from Devon is friendship and nothing more,* she told herself.

When she entered the classroom, Elizabeth immediately spotted Devon sitting at their lab table. He had already pulled a stool over for her and had started setting things up. She pulled her hair behind her shoulders and tugged at the bottom of her blue cotton vest.

"Howdy, partner," Devon said as Elizabeth approached. In faded blue jeans and a snug-fitting black T-shirt with a crew neck, Devon was looking even cuter than he had the day before. Elizabeth felt a flutter of excitement in her stomach.

He's just a friend, she reminded herself.

"So what is it today?" she asked, noticing the small beaker of pale green liquid in Devon's hand. "Are you going to astonish me by producing my exact hair color in there?"

"Mixing colors is yesterday's news," he answered confidently. "Today we're on to bigger and better things."

"I can hardly wait," Elizabeth replied, her eyes sparkling with interest. "But I do have one question for you." She tried to put a sober expression on her face as she looked at him.

"Shoot," Devon responded quickly, becoming serious.

"If you keep coming up with all of these tricks for me, exactly when do you propose we finish the labs Mr. Russo assigns us?" Elizabeth asked in mock consternation.

"Is that all?" Devon asked in a cavalier tone. "Don't worry about it. We've got plenty of time for both. Today we're just supposed to finish up the lab from yesterday, which we finished early anyway. And if I'm a halfway decent judge of character, I'd guess you wrote up your report last night, just like I did."

Elizabeth blushed. She was never one to put off work until the next day. Devon was right. She had indeed finished writing up the lab already— although it had been hard with him invading her thoughts constantly.

"As for the rest of the week," Devon continued, "I looked ahead at the lab schedule. There aren't any assignments that will take us the entire period, so it looks like you're in for at least twenty minutes of stupid Devon tricks all week long."

Elizabeth laughed, glad to hear that Devon was going to continue with his fascinating experiments. They were far more interesting than anything described in Elizabeth's immense textbook.

"It sounds like you've got everything covered," Elizabeth said happily. "So what are we up to today?" Devon grinned and held out the small flask for Elizabeth to see.

"In my hand I hold a solution that can communicate volumes without saying a word," he proclaimed with a great flourish of his hand.

Elizabeth furrowed her brow, attempting to figure out his riddle.

"Communicate volumes . . . ," she repeated slowly, drumming her fingers on the table. "I'd guess that you somehow dissolved an encyclopedia

67

set in there," she joked, "but I think that would require much more liquid."

"Not bad," Devon responded, raising his eyebrows. "But not correct either. Ms. Wakefield, today I present you with invisible ink." He held up a cotton swab for her inspection. "And with this ink, I intend to write you a secret message."

He dipped the swab in the green liquid and began writing with it on a blank piece of paper. Elizabeth watched him work, but he turned his back to her slightly so that she couldn't make out the letters. After a minute he raised the paper to his lips and blew delicately on it to help it dry. Then he passed the paper to Elizabeth.

She picked it up and examined both sides of it. The paper was completely blank, without even a trace of color. She looked at Devon, puzzled.

"This is great," she said, gesturing to the paper, "but now what am I supposed to do?"

Devon smiled slyly. "I'm afraid it's up to you," he said. Elizabeth was still confused. "But I will tell you that right here in front of you is everything necessary to create a solution that will make the message appear."

Elizabeth was intrigued. *What a great experiment,* she thought. *I never knew chemistry could be so much fun.*

"OK," she responded. "How much time do we have?"

Devon glanced at the clock. "Still a good forty minutes left in class," he informed her.

"No sweat," Elizabeth said confidently. "I'll have it done in thirty," she boasted.

Devon laughed and shook his head. "You're something else," he said, still grinning.

Elizabeth looked up at him briefly. "I'll take that as a compliment," she returned. "And you're not so bad yourself."

Devon actually blushed. *He is* so *cute,* Elizabeth thought.

"Now stop distracting me," she chided. "I have work to do." Devon laughed again. Elizabeth immediately got down to business, examining the various materials in front of her as well as the remaining invisible ink.

Devon started to offer her hints a few times, but she insisted on figuring things out herself. She instructed him that he was only to help her if she asked a specific question, and even then she didn't want him to do anything but answer exactly what she had asked.

"I thought I was in charge here." Devon sighed. "You sure are demanding."

"You have to be demanding in order to survive in my family," Elizabeth responded, still working intently. "When you're a twin, people tend to think of the two of you as one person unless you speak up for yourself."

"I wouldn't know about that," Devon replied seriously. Elizabeth looked up at him again.

"Do you have any brothers or sisters?" she inquired. Devon shifted on his stool.

"Nope," he responded. "I'm an only child."

"I guess that means your parents probably spoiled you rotten when you were little, huh?" Elizabeth teased. Right away she sensed she had said something wrong. Devon tensed a little and hesitated as though he wasn't sure how to respond.

"I'm sorry," Elizabeth added quickly. "I've obviously said something that upset you." Devon looked at her soberly, gazing deep into her eyes. Almost immediately Elizabeth saw his face relax, and he looked at her warmly.

"No, it's OK," he said reassuringly. "I don't mind talking to you about it."

Elizabeth stared at him, not knowing what to expect.

"My parents died in a car crash about a month ago," Devon began.

"Oh, no," Elizabeth gasped. She looked into his eyes searchingly. "I'm so sorry; I didn't—" She was stumbling to apologize when he cut her off.

"Don't worry about it," he said, but Elizabeth felt horrible. How could she have been so stupid?

"It's really all right," he continued. "I know it must sound strange, but things have actually worked out for the best." He paused and looked at Elizabeth with a sincere expression. She held his gaze patiently, waiting for him to continue. It seemed that he wanted to talk about it, and she intended to listen for as long as he wanted.

"I was never very close to my parents," he said. "So as odd as it may sound, I wasn't really devastated by their deaths. In fact . . ." He hesitated again. "I almost feel guilty saying it, but my life seems to be better now. More normal."

Elizabeth blinked a few times and bit her lip. *It must have been horrible for him to grow up without ever really loving his parents,* she thought. *And no brothers or sisters either. How lonely.*

"Now I live with a woman named Nan Johnstone," he continued. "She was my nanny when I was younger, and she practically raised me." Devon smiled warmly, and Elizabeth knew instantly that Nan meant a lot to him.

"She was more of a parent to me than my mother and father ever were," he said.

"Wow," was all Elizabeth could think to say at first. "You've really been through a lot lately. I'd never have guessed; I m-mean . . . you seem so well-adjusted," she stammered. Devon chuckled. Elizabeth looked down and shook her head. She was embarrassed at how tactless she must have sounded.

"I *am* well-adjusted," Devon responded, smiling. Then he placed his hand lightly on her chin. A tingling sensation rushed through her body when he touched her. She felt as though she were floating in midair. As she swallowed back a gasp Devon raised her chin so that she was looking at him.

"But you're not going to be doing so well if you don't get to work," he jested. His words brought her back down to earth. Elizabeth straightened up on her stool.

"Good point," she acknowledged, looking at her watch. She returned to the materials in front of her but couldn't help thinking about what Devon had just told her. He had shared important personal information with her, and she was flattered. She felt closer to him now than she had just ten minutes ago. It was funny. She had only known him for two days, but she already felt like she could talk to him about anything. Obviously he felt the same way.

Enough messing around, she told herself. *Back to the task at hand.*

Once again she began mixing and testing various combinations of liquids. Elizabeth was in her element. She loved the process of putting clues together to solve a mystery, and she thoroughly enjoyed a good challenge. She knew that working with Devon was encouraging her to develop her already keen powers of analysis even further. In just a short time he had opened her mind to entirely new ways of thinking, and she welcomed the adventure. With Devon she didn't know what to expect next, and she found it thrilling.

Suddenly Elizabeth sat up straight in her seat. "I think I've got it!" she exclaimed. She grabbed the piece of paper Devon had given her and began slowly applying the potion she had concocted.

Sure enough, letters, and then entire words, began to appear in front of her. When she had coated the whole page with her solution, she held it up to read. Elizabeth felt her pulse speed up. She was astounded to find that Devon had written her a note asking her to go out on a date.

Conflicting emotions overcame her. All at once she was excited, happy, and filled with guilt. She couldn't deny that she wanted to accept the invitation, and she was aware that a part of her had hoped he would express an interest in her that went beyond friendship. But she also knew that there was no way she could say yes.

Elizabeth sat staring at the note for a moment and then finally looked up at Devon. He was waiting expectantly. She felt a wave of disappointment run through her body as she spoke to him.

"This is really nice, and I'm flattered," she said quietly. "But I'm afraid I can't accept." Devon's excited smile wilted, and he looked as though she had just punched him in the gut. Elizabeth's heart broke in sympathy.

"It's not you," Elizabeth added quickly. "It's just that . . ." She was reluctant to continue, but finally she managed to get the words out. "I already have a boyfriend."

Devon looked away, saying nothing.

"His name is Todd Wilkins," she added, trying to fill the awkward silence. "We've been seeing each other for a while. He's, um . . . really . . . uh . . . nice," she stammered, not sure what else to say. Devon fidgeted with his pen and continued to look down. Elizabeth could see that she was only making matters worse. Then she remembered her conversation with Jessica from the previous night.

"Besides," Elizabeth said. "I thought you were supposed to go out with Jessica for a grand tour of Sweet Valley."

"Oh, yeah," Devon said without raising his eyes. "Well . . ."

He didn't finish the sentence. Elizabeth sensed he wasn't as excited about the tour as Jessica had implied. She tried to think of something else to say but thankfully was saved by the bell. As they got up to leave she caught Devon's eye.

"I am sorry," she said sincerely. He looked into her eyes, and his expression softened.

"I know," he said solemnly. "I understand." Then he perked up a little. "See you in class tomorrow?" Elizabeth knew he was trying to tell her everything would be fine. She smiled warmly back at him.

"Can't wait," she answered.

Devon turned and walked out in front of her. When Elizabeth got to the door, she spied Jessica waiting casually across the hall. Elizabeth knew that Jessica's first class had been French, which was on the other side of the school. It was obvious Jessica had planned to be waiting outside Mr. Russo's room when the bell rang so that she could "accidentally" bump into Devon. She watched enviously as Jessica fell into step with him.

Elizabeth knew she had done the right thing by turning down Devon's invitation. It would have been wrong for her to do anything else. Still, she couldn't help but notice that doing the right thing felt pretty lousy in this case.

At lunchtime Devon exited through the courtyard door and began walking over to the shady spot next to the tree where he had lounged the day before. Earlier in the day both Winston and Jessica had invited him to join them at their tables, but Devon enjoyed eating alone. It gave him time to think things over in peace.

Right now all he wanted to do was figure out a way to win Elizabeth's heart.

As he approached his spot Devon caught a glimpse of shiny blond hair. At first he thought it was Elizabeth, and his heart soared—maybe she had changed her mind about the date. But as he got closer to the tree he realized that it was just Jessica. It was the outfit that gave it away.

Jessica was wearing a lime-colored tank top over a slim-fitting miniskirt of the same color. Her square-heeled sandals had matching lime-colored patent leather straps, and they made her long legs look even longer. She wore a brightly colored beaded necklace and matching earrings that complemented the outfit. Devon had to admit that she looked attractive, but she was too trendy for his taste.

Jessica was talking to one of her friends, and Devon thought he might be able to avoid eye contact and make a quick getaway. But before he could turn to go, Jessica was waving for him to join them.

It's almost like she was waiting for me, Devon thought, reluctantly joining the girls under the tree. Jessica wasted no time.

"Devon, this is my friend Lila Fowler," she said. "Lila, this is Devon." Oddly Jessica sounded like a proud parent introducing her honors-student son or something. She was literally beaming.

"It's very nice to meet you, Devon," Lila said politely. "Jessica has told me a *great deal* about you," she added, glancing at her friend with a mischievous smile.

Jessica's features tightened at Lila's ribbing, and Devon smirked. He liked this Lila girl already.

"It's nice to meet you too," Devon returned, looking directly into Lila's brown eyes. He couldn't help noticing that she was an attractive girl. Her wavy, chestnut brown hair cascaded softly down to her shoulders, contrasting with her ivory silk top and coordinating skirt. The outfit accentuated her smooth, tan complexion and gave her skin a healthy glow.

Lila easily met Devon's gaze as they shook hands. She seemed incredibly poised for a girl her age—and wealthy.

When he let her hand drop from his grasp, he noticed the gold-and-ruby ring on her fourth finger. Devon had seen enough expensive jewelry on his mother and her friends to know that Lila's ring was no fake. *A girl my parents would have been proud to have me date,* he thought ruefully.

"So where are you from, Devon?" Lila asked courteously while Jessica looked on. Devon hesitated. He had hoped to excuse himself before anyone could start a conversation, but it was too late now.

"Connecticut," he answered plainly. Lila perked up instantly.

"Interesting. I have an aunt who lives in Connecticut. What section are you from?" she asked, tilting her head. Devon saw Jessica roll her eyes. She seemed upset that Lila was monopolizing the conversation.

"I grew up in Westwood," Devon replied casually. Lila raised her eyebrows at the mention of Devon's hometown.

"Really?" she responded, sounding impressed. "That's a rather exclusive area, isn't it?" At this question Jessica's eyes widened as well. She didn't seem annoyed with Lila anymore. She seemed eager for more information.

Devon didn't want to let on that he came from a wealthy background. People inevitably began to treat him differently once they found out about his money.

"It can't be too exclusive," he joked. "After all, they let me in." Lila laughed quietly at his remark but narrowed her eyes. Devon suspected that she was still curious about his family and any possible connections to wealth.

"I have to run," he said before she could quiz him further. "I just remembered that I'm supposed to meet with Mr. Farrington today to talk about my schedule. He wanted me to stop in and let him know how things are going." It wasn't a complete lie. After all, Mr. Farrington *had* asked Devon to check in. He just hadn't set up a specific appointment.

"That's too bad," Jessica said, looking disappointed.

Sometimes Devon was surprised by how well he could lie and how easily he could manipulate people. It concerned him a little at times, but he had to admit, it came in handy.

"Maybe I'll catch you after school," Jessica added, smiling flirtatiously. "I still owe you a tour of the town."

"Right," he responded without enthusiasm. He knew that Jessica wanted him to take her up on the offer, but he just wasn't interested. *If she promised to bring Elizabeth along, I might consider it,* Devon thought remorsefully. "I can't do it today, but maybe some other time."

His heart turned when he noticed the crestfallen look on Jessica's face. He hated to hurt her feelings, but—for obvious reasons—he couldn't even look at Jessica without thinking of Elizabeth. And he needed some time alone to figure out what his next move should be.

"It was nice to meet you, Lila," Devon said sincerely. She nodded. Then he turned to Jessica briefly. "Catch ya later."

"Yeah. Later," Jessica said softly.

Devon managed a smile before he turned to walk back to the school.

That was a close one, he thought, putting distance between himself and the two girls.

It wasn't that he didn't like them—Jessica was nice enough, and Lila, though obviously a bit stuck-up, had seemed OK too. She struck Devon as rather intelligent and witty, and she was definitely much more refined than Jessica. In fact, if he could get past her snobbery, he might even enjoy hanging out with her.

But as for Jessica, he just couldn't seem to avoid her. She seemed to show up everywhere he went. She was always waiting right outside his classes to walk him to his next period, and now she was showing up at lunch too. Devon wanted to believe that it was accidental or that Jessica was just being friendly, but it seemed pretty obvious she had something else in mind.

It wasn't that the thought of dating Jessica hadn't crossed his mind. After all, he couldn't have Elizabeth, and Jessica *was* her identical twin. But it just wouldn't feel right.

She's pretty lucky I'm a nice guy, he told himself. He knew plenty of boys back in Connecticut who would just go out with her whether they cared for her or not. It was obvious that she'd jump at the chance to date him if he just asked her. But that wasn't Devon's style.

He knew that dating Jessica just because Elizabeth had turned him down would be unfair— to Jessica and to himself. Devon despised people who used others in any way. He knew he could never behave that way himself.

No, he thought. *Regardless of what Jessica Wakefield may be up to, I know I could never take advantage of her.*

Chapter 6

Elizabeth sat at the computer in the *Oracle* office after school, attempting to finish her column. The place was totally deserted, but Elizabeth didn't mind because she wasn't getting any work done as it was. If there were people around, she would be totally useless.

She drummed her fingers on the keyboard, trying to form her next sentence in her head. Suddenly the door to the office swung open. Elizabeth was startled.

"What's wrong with me?" Jessica asked, standing in the doorway with her arms extended from her sides.

Elizabeth looked over Jessica's green outfit and platforms and pretended to ponder the question.

"Hmmm . . . where should I begin?" Elizabeth joked.

"Very funny," Jessica sneered, wrinkling her nose. She walked into the office and flopped down on the couch along the wall.

"What I mean," Jessica continued indignantly, "is that I have given Devon Whitelaw every possible opportunity to ask me out, and he hasn't even broached the subject yet." Jessica looked at her sister pleadingly. "So what am I doing wrong?"

Elizabeth felt herself blushing and hoped it wasn't noticeable. *Apparently what you're doing wrong is you're not me,* Elizabeth thought wryly.

But she knew she couldn't tell Jessica about Devon's invisible ink note. As much as Elizabeth hated to keep anything from her twin, she knew that Jessica would only be hurt or jealous.

"He *is* new, Jess," she said finally. "Maybe he's a little shy about asking someone out right away." Jessica looked hopeful but not convinced.

"Do you think so?" she asked Elizabeth.

"Absolutely," Elizabeth lied. "Especially someone like you. You're so popular, and it's obvious that a lot of guys like you. He might even think you already have a boyfriend," she added, noting the irony of her statement.

"That's true," Jessica said thoughtfully. "Of course he would assume someone like me is already attached."

Elizabeth had to focus in order to keep from rolling her eyes.

"Besides, he's been through a lot lately," she said matter-of-factly. "I'm sure he has trouble opening up a little." Elizabeth realized she had gone too far with her last statement as soon as it was out of her mouth. Jessica's eyes narrowed, and she tilted her head suspiciously.

"How do you know he's been through a lot?" she asked. "Did he tell you something?"

Elizabeth thought quickly.

"Yes, I mean no, I mean—*he* didn't, but Mr. Russo said Devon had been through a lot when he was asking me if I'd be his lab partner." Elizabeth bit her tongue. She knew she had covered up her first mistake successfully, but now she had let it slip that she was Devon's lab partner. She hadn't mentioned it to Jessica before and didn't want her sister to question her about it now.

Thankfully Jessica seemed satisfied with her explanation and didn't even ask about the two of them being lab partners. Elizabeth sighed, relieved.

Jessica sat up straight and leaned forward. She gazed intently at Elizabeth, clearly getting ready to ask a favor. Elizabeth patiently awaited her twin's request, already dreading it. She had a hunch she knew what Jessica wanted.

"I was thinking, Liz," Jessica began in her

sweetest voice, "since you have chemistry with Devon, do you think you could put in a good word for me? You know, talk about my good features?" She flashed her perfect smile and tilted her head upward.

The last thing Elizabeth wanted to do right now was set Jessica up with Devon. She knew that if they got together, she would just about die of envy. But what possible reason could she have for turning down Jessica's request?

"I'll try," Elizabeth finally managed. "But I don't know how much good it will do. I don't know him very well," she lied. "I barely get to talk to him at all."

"Thanks, Lizzie," Jessica gushed, refusing to be deterred. She bounded over to the desk to give her sister a quick hug. "You're the greatest!"

"No problem," Elizabeth mumbled grumpily.

Jessica stopped at the door and turned to face Elizabeth again.

"Oh—I almost forgot," she said. "Can I use your computer at home to surf the Net later? I have a little research to do."

Elizabeth was astonished. "*You* do research?" she asked her twin in disbelief. Jessica grinned devilishly.

"I have one more trick I haven't tried with our illustrious Mr. Whitelaw yet," she confided.

"Something that he shouldn't be able to resist."

Elizabeth shook her head. "I should have known," she told Jessica. "It figures that the one time you decide to get on-line it's because of a guy."

"Can you think of a better reason?" Jessica asked jovially. She turned and skipped out into the hallway, not bothering to wait for an answer.

Elizabeth couldn't help laughing. If nothing else, she had to admit Jessica was determined.

She turned back to her computer, intending to finish her article, but she was distracted by a queasy feeling in the pit of her stomach. She tried to let the feeling go, but she couldn't. There was no use fighting it. She was envious of Jessica.

It's not fair, she thought. Elizabeth knew she shouldn't be jealous, but she couldn't help it. Devon was a great guy, and he had asked *her* out, not Jessica.

Get a grip, Liz, she told herself. *You've already got a boyfriend.* She tried to convince herself that Jessica dating Devon would be for the best. Elizabeth knew she had to let go of her inappropriate feelings for Devon.

She forced herself to put her emotions aside and get back to work. Tomorrow she would do her best to convince Devon that Jessica would be a great girlfriend for him, and that was that. After all, it was the right thing to do.

*   *   *

86

Todd pulled into the Sweet Valley High student parking lot in his black BMW on Wednesday morning. He was at school much earlier than usual, but then, he had serious business to attend to.

He stepped out of his car and looked around the lot. Sure enough, there was Jessica standing on the pathway between the parking area and the school. Right where he had expected her to be. And thankfully Elizabeth was nowhere in sight. Todd knew Elizabeth would be at her weekly staff meeting for the *Oracle*, and he had decided to take the opportunity to try to catch Jessica alone.

He walked over to Jessica, who was busily watching the entrance to the drive. She was so focused, she didn't even see him approach.

"Boo!" Todd shouted when he was just a foot away from her. Jessica jumped and turned around quickly.

"Todd!" she whined. "You scared me! What're you doing here at this hour?"

Todd smiled. "I'd ask you the same question," he kidded, "but I know exactly what you're doing." Jessica was wearing an extra-short blue plaid miniskirt topped with a midriff-baring sleeveless white shirt. The outfit drew attention to her slim waist and fit stomach and would certainly catch the eyes of most of the guys at SVH.

But Todd knew there was only one guy Jessica

87

wanted attention from these days—that new guy, Devon Whitelaw. Todd hadn't met him yet, but he had seen Jessica waiting in the same spot on Monday and Tuesday morning and guessed that she would continue to be there each day until Devon was wrapped tightly around her finger.

"So how are things with you and your hunky biker stud?" he teased.

"Fine," Jessica stated flatly, ignoring Todd's playful jibe. "He's coming around, and I'm sure we'll be on our first date soon."

"You mean you haven't been out on a date yet?" Todd asked, feigning shock. "It's been five whole days since you first saw him, Jess! Are you losing your touch?"

Jessica turned away from Todd and began searching the driveway again. Todd sensed he had hit a sore subject.

He would have enjoyed rubbing it in to Jessica that for once she wasn't getting her way, but he didn't want to upset her when he was about to ask her for a favor. He decided it would be best not to pry into her love life any further right now.

"Listen," he said. "I need to talk to you about a surprise I have planned for Elizabeth." Jessica turned around and eyed Todd suspiciously.

"And just what do you need from me?" she asked.

Todd raised one eyebrow and grinned. "Now that you mention it," he began, "I could use your help." Jessica waved her hand and rolled her eyes, signaling for him to get on with it. It was obvious her mind was on other things.

"I'm planning a little celebration for Elizabeth because of the big occasion that's coming up," Todd said, certain that Elizabeth must have mentioned to her twin that it had been almost one year since she had become a published writer. Jessica furrowed her brow.

"What on earth are you talking about?" she demanded, tapping her foot impatiently.

"You mean Elizabeth hasn't said anything to you about her anniversary?" Todd inquired, readjusting his backpack on his shoulder. Jessica exhaled heavily.

"Come on, Todd." She groaned. "I don't have time for this. *What* anniversary?"

Todd looked back at Jessica, who was staring at him with her arms crossed over her chest and her head cocked. *If looks could kill, I'd be sporting some pretty serious injuries right now,* Todd thought. He decided he had better fill her in.

"Next Monday will be the one-year anniversary of the day that Liz had her first article published in the *Oracle.* I can't believe she hasn't said anything to you about it." Jessica's expression softened slightly.

"That does sound like the kind of thing Liz would get all excited about." She considered it for a moment and then shrugged in a dismissive gesture.

"She's been really busy with the *Oracle* lately," she offered in explanation. "I'm sure it just slipped her mind."

"I guess so," Todd answered, nodding. It wasn't like Elizabeth to forget special dates, but Jessica was probably right. He swung his backpack down to the ground by his feet and then pulled at the bottom of his white T-shirt and green fleece vest to straighten them.

"Anyway," Todd continued, "getting back to the surprise . . . I was wondering if you could help me pick out a present for Elizabeth."

"You want me to help you shop?" Jessica asked with interest. "I guess I could do that. After all, shopping *is* one of my personal strengths."

"Great," Todd said appreciatively. "But there's more. I need you to put one of your other stellar talents to work too."

"And what might that be?" Jessica asked, narrowing her eyes again.

"Scheming," Todd answered, raising his eyebrows twice in rapid succession. Jessica smirked.

"I need you to get Elizabeth to the beach next Monday at four o'clock in the afternoon without letting her know what's going on," Todd explained.

"Plotting against my own sister?" Jessica asked with false innocence. "What kind of person do you think I am?"

"You *are* Jessica Wakefield, aren't you?" Todd joked. "Or do I have the wrong twin?" Jessica laughed.

"Normally I would have to say no to such trickery," she quipped flirtatiously, "but I'm a sucker for romance."

"Thanks for making such a sacrifice, Jess," Todd said sarcastically. Jessica put her hand over her heart and feigned a noble expression.

"Anything for love," she said comically. "Besides, Liz is helping me with a little love project of my own."

"Really?" Todd asked.

"She has chemistry class with Devon, so she's going to talk to him and put in a good word for me," Jessica explained.

Todd was caught off guard.

"I didn't know Devon was in Elizabeth's chemistry class," he said. "She didn't mention anything about him."

"Oh, you know Liz," Jessica said with another shrug. "She's so in love with you, she wouldn't notice another cute guy if he showed up on our doorstep with flowers."

91

Todd started to laugh, but then he noticed Jessica suddenly stiffening. She began adjusting her skirt and running her hands through her hair. Before Todd had time to blink, Jessica turned to give him a little push, moving him off to the side.

"Hey!" Todd uttered indignantly, catching his balance.

"Here he comes," Jessica said excitedly. "You've got to get out of here. I want to be alone with him, and I don't need him seeing me with other guys. He might think you're my boyfriend or something."

Todd laughed out loud at Jessica's frenzied movements, and she shot him a menacing look. He glanced down the driveway to see a motorcycle approaching from the far end. Then he turned back to Jessica, who was still preening.

"Boy, this guy's really got you jumping," he mused. Jessica glared at him.

"Just go," she said quickly, waving her hands as if to brush him away. Todd moved closer to her and put his arm around her shoulders.

"Oh, come on, Jess," he whined, pretending to be hurt. "I thought we were buddies. Don't you want to introduce me to your new friend?" Jessica threw his arm off her shoulders and pushed him away more forcefully this time.

"Get out of here!" she barked.

"But you're going to help me with Liz, right?" he asked, backing away slowly.

"Yes!" she yelled, waving him off.

"So we'll go shopping Friday after school?" he persisted as the motorcycle neared them.

"Sure—whatever!" Jessica snapped. "Just get out of here!"

Todd knew he had pushed her far enough. He gave her one last amused grin and headed toward the school.

Chapter 7

"Phew!" Elizabeth sighed, rushing into chemistry class just as the bell rang. "I didn't think I was going to make it on time," she said, taking her seat next to Devon.

"What happened? Did you oversleep this morning?" he asked, greeting her with his usual warm smile.

"Not exactly," Elizabeth responded, still catching her breath. "I had a meeting that ran a little late, and I had to run to make it here on time." She rummaged through her backpack while she spoke, then dropped it to the floor in exasperation. Closing her eyes, she took a deep breath, trying to calm herself.

"What's the matter?" Devon asked, sounding concerned but mildly amused.

94

"Just that I'm totally scatterbrained," she said, looking up at him. "I forgot to grab my books in advance, and I left my notebook at the meeting." She checked her pockets quickly.

"Ugh," she groaned, "I don't even have a pen. I hate days that start this way. I can't stand being disorganized."

Devon looked at her sympathetically and put his hand on her shoulder. He stared directly into her eyes.

"OK, Liz. Focus. You're gonna have to calm down before your head explodes," he said with a half smile. "I happen to like that beautiful face of yours exactly where it is."

Elizabeth stared back at him, feeling an intense blush rise from her toes all the way to her scalp.

"Maybe I can help put you in a better mood," he offered.

Can't he tell he already has? Elizabeth wondered.

Without another word Devon opened his notebook and took out an extra pen, which he handed to Elizabeth. She grinned and opened her mouth to thank him, but he held up one finger to silence her.

Next he pulled apart his three-ring binder and extracted a spiral-bound notebook, which he also gave to Elizabeth. Once again she tried to thank him, but for a second time he held up his hand, indicating that she should wait. Elizabeth laughed and shook her head.

She watched silently as Devon reached to the shelf behind him. He moved a microscope to the side and retrieved a small beaker. It was full of paper flowers. Elizabeth gasped when she saw it.

"Those are beautiful," she exclaimed. The flowers were arranged in the beaker like a bouquet. Each was made of bright, rainbow-colored tissue paper and had a dark green wire stem. Devon placed the "vase" in front of Elizabeth, and she noticed that there was a small card attached. It read simply: For Elizabeth. She was stunned.

"When did you do this?" she asked, amazed.

"I was here a little early today," Devon said, shrugging off the gesture nonchalantly. Elizabeth could tell just by looking, though, that he had obviously spent a great deal of time on them. They were very intricately designed and positively exquisite. Devon was definitely being modest. As usual.

"I thought you might like them," he added. Elizabeth didn't know what to say.

This guy is too good to be true, she thought. *He's so thoughtful.* Once again Devon had managed to start off her school day by making her absolutely swoon. She was speechless.

"I realize they're not exactly hothouse flowers," Devon said, waking Elizabeth from her astonished state. "In fact, I guess they're actually 'chem lab' flowers, but I hope they help improve your day a little."

"How could they not?" she gushed. "They're absolutely gorgeous. Thank you so much."

"You're welcome," Devon said, smiling. "And don't worry. There's a little chemistry lesson here. If you did your homework last night, you know we're about to study chromatics—the science of color—so I thought these rainbow-colored flowers would be appropriate."

Elizabeth was riveted by the intensity in his eyes. He was the most considerate guy she had ever met, and definitely the most creative. *And the most intelligent, and handsome, and kind,* she thought. The list of Devon's positive qualities was growing longer by the minute.

"You realize you're far too good to me, don't you?" Elizabeth finally said.

"Absolutely," Devon answered, grinning. "But we can talk about that later. Why don't you take a deep breath, relax, and tell me what your meeting was about."

Elizabeth was glad he had changed the subject so quickly. Sometimes she got so caught up in Devon that she forgot about the rest of the world.

Although she had to admit she enjoyed the feeling, she couldn't help worrying that her thoughts were inappropriate, and she welcomed the return to reality.

"It was just a staff meeting for the *Oracle*," she told him. "I contribute a few articles each week and author a regular column."

"So you like to write?" he asked.

"I *love* to write," Elizabeth corrected him. "Someday I hope to make a living as a writer. A novelist or a journalist . . . I'm not sure exactly. But definitely something centered around writing." Devon was clearly impressed.

"I think it's great that you have something you're so passionate about," he said. "I'd love to read some of your stuff sometime—if you don't mind."

"I wouldn't mind at all," Elizabeth replied, beaming. She was flattered that he had taken such an interest in something so important to her.

Being around Devon made her feel vibrant, like each word she said was vital. He was genuinely interested in her and the things that she did, and the feeling was mutual. She found him captivating.

Suddenly Elizabeth remembered that she was supposed to be talking about Jessica. She would have preferred to continue their current conversation, but she had promised her sister. She tried to change the subject subtly.

"Writing is my favorite pastime, but it means that I end up spending a lot of time cooped up in my room," Elizabeth said, staring at the ground. Then she forced herself to look up into Devon's eyes and sound enthused. "I'm the complete opposite of Jessica. She's always on the go, and she's involved in so many things. Did you know that she's a cocaptain of the cheerleading squad?"

"Yeah," Devon answered. "I saw her on her way to practice after school yesterday. I think she mentioned something about being a captain." He didn't sound impressed. Elizabeth decided to play it up some more.

"You should see her at some of the games. She's incredible," Elizabeth said with exaggerated enthusiasm. "A lot of people credit her for the fact that our crowds show such spirit. The guys on the football and basketball teams say that she can single-handedly turn a game around when they're losing."

"I'm not a big cheerleading fan," he said, obviously disinterested. "Are you into sports at all?"

"Me?" Elizabeth asked. She thought for a moment. "I've always enjoyed tennis, but I can never get anyone to play with me. Jessica's always too busy with cheering, and Todd would rather play basketball with the guys."

"Really?" he asked, sitting up straighter and leaning forward. "I love tennis. I used to play all the time in Connecticut. Maybe we could play after school sometime."

"That would be great," Elizabeth said, excited, but she stopped herself from pursuing the idea. She knew she had to try to bring the conversation back to Jessica.

"But you should spend some time getting to know Sweet Valley first," Elizabeth said, thinking fast. "It's really a beautiful town, and I know Jessica offered to play tour guide for you—you should take her up on it. She's so much fun to be around. There's never a dull moment."

"Yeah. Somehow I sensed that already," Devon said blandly. He was looking down again, doodling on the cover of his marble-faced notebook.

"She could really show you an exciting night on the town," Elizabeth said, refusing to be deterred. "I prefer to sit at home and rent an old movie or something boring like that."

"Are you kidding?" Devon responded. "That's not boring at all. I *love* old movies. *Casablanca*, *Rebel Without a Cause*. How could you call that boring?"

Elizabeth smiled. Those were two of her favorite movies. In fact, Devon reminded her a bit of James Dean's character in *Rebel*. He was so cool and beyond sexy. She blushed at her own thoughts.

"I didn't say that *I* thought they were boring,"

Elizabeth corrected, trying not to look flustered. "It's just that other people don't usually think of watching an old movie as an exciting way to spend a Saturday night."

"Other people like who?" Devon asked. "Jessica?"

"No," Elizabeth lied. How could she salvage this situation? "Not Jessica . . . a—a lot of people."

Elizabeth realized she wasn't doing much to help her sister's cause. She forced herself to make one last effort.

"It's just that Jessica prefers to be involved in the action instead of sitting back and watching it. She's practically a movie star herself," Elizabeth continued. "She can walk into any room and instantly become the center of attention. It's funny, we look exactly alike, but people pay a lot more attention to her—even when we enter a room *together*. She definitely has a star quality about her."

"Yeah," Devon said, nodding. "I've noticed the way people really flock to her. She always seems to be surrounded by a crowd."

Finally, Elizabeth thought, *I said something about Jess that interested him.* But her relief was only temporary.

"Personally I try to avoid crowds altogether," Devon added. "I prefer anonymity. A quiet night at home suits me just fine." *Just like me,* Elizabeth thought. She felt like jumping for joy that she and Devon had so much in common and kicking herself at the same time.

Jessica would kill me if she heard how this conversation was going, Elizabeth thought. *But it's not like I'm misrepresenting her.* Elizabeth decided she had better stop before she made things even worse.

"Whoa, it's already eight o'clock," she said, glancing at her watch. "We better get down to business and start writing the hypothesis for today's lab." Devon looked up at the clock and raised his eyebrows.

"I guess you're right," he agreed. "We don't want to fall behind, or I won't have time to show you how I made the flowers." He shot a sly smile at Elizabeth, then grabbed a piece of paper from his notebook and started writing.

Elizabeth picked up the pen he had given her and flipped to a blank page in the notebook, but she couldn't help looking up to observe Devon. He was intent on his work and didn't even notice her staring.

Whenever she looked at him, her heart pounded furiously and her palms started to sweat. There were butterflies dancing in her stomach as she thought about how alike she and Devon were—how they almost seemed to be made for each other. Suddenly she knew that she had not only failed her sister, but she was failing Todd too. She couldn't fight it any longer. She wanted to be with Devon—big time.

Elizabeth tried to push her feelings aside, but she couldn't. Devon was perfect. And no matter how she looked at it, Todd seemed to be just like all the other guys—always off shooting hoops or watching sports on TV.

Chocolate cake batter spattered the walls of the Wilkinses' spacious kitchen.

Todd yelped, holding the electric mixer away from his body. The beaters were still turning on high speed, coating the front of his shirt and his face with chocolate. Finally, unable to find the right button to turn off the mixer, Todd resorted to pulling the plug from the outlet.

"Oh, man," he said out loud, looking around the room. He had been attempting a test run of some of Elizabeth's favorite foods, but so far all he had done was make a mess of the kitchen.

There was flour all over the countertop and on the floor, along with cocoa powder, sugar, and some dried egg. He had tried to melt some butter in the microwave, but he had left it in its plastic container with the cover on. It had exploded, leaving the oven door covered with a greasy mess.

Todd squinted, looking at the batter that remained inside the mixing bowl. It was a muddy dark brown, almost black in color, which didn't seem quite right. He stuck in a reluctant finger and brought it to his lips. As soon as he tasted it Todd had the urge to spit it out. He grabbed a dishcloth and wiped at his tongue frantically.

"Yuck!" he exclaimed, throwing the cloth into the sink. "This is terrible," he muttered to himself, examining his surroundings. "It's definitely time to call in the reinforcements."

He grabbed the cordless phone, which was also coated in chocolate, and dialed Enid's phone number. Enid Rollins was one of Elizabeth's best friends and also an excellent cook. When Todd had mentioned to her that he planned to cook for Elizabeth's celebration, she had offered to prepare the food for him. But Todd had insisted that he wanted to serve Elizabeth food he had made for her himself. Now, however, he was beginning to wish he had taken her up on her offer. When he got Enid on the phone, he wasted no time with small talk.

"OK," he began without even saying hello, "I followed the recipe exactly, so why does my chocolate cake batter taste like dirt?"

"Having a little trouble, are we, Chef Wilkins?" Enid asked with a laugh.

"Very funny, Rollins," Todd responded flatly. "But what do you think I did wrong?"

"I'm not sure," Enid replied slowly. "Exactly what does the batter taste like—and don't say dirt. You know, is it too sweet, too bitter? Try to describe it."

Todd remembered the taste in his mouth and winced. "It's definitely too bitter," he answered. "But I put in a centimeter of sugar, just like the recipe said, so I don't—"

"Wait a second," Enid interrupted. "You put in a *centimeter* of sugar? Exactly what do you mean by that?"

"Just what I said," Todd answered. "A centimeter. The recipe says one centimeter of sugar." Enid laughed uncontrollably.

"What?" Todd demanded, feeling defensive.

"Do you have the cookbook in front of you?" she asked through her laughter, obviously trying to regain her composure.

"Yeah, why?" Todd questioned.

"Just read me the ingredients," Enid instructed him. "All of them."

Todd flipped open the cookbook to the cake section, where he had found the recipe, and began to list the ingredients.

"Five ounces of bittersweet chocolate, one and a half sticks of butter, three eggs, three egg yolks,

105

one centimeter of sugar—" Enid interrupted him again, obviously stifling a laugh.

"Does it actually *say* centimeter, Todd, or is there just a lowercase *c* next to the sugar?"

"There's just a *c*," Todd answered, "but—" Once again he was cut off by Enid's hysterical laughter.

"That stands for *cup*, Todd." She giggled. "Not centimeter."

Todd felt a sudden wave of embarrassment rush over him, quickly followed by a feeling of hopelessness. *How am I ever going to get this right?* he asked himself. When Enid had finally stopped giggling, she apologized.

"I'm sorry, Todd," she said, still catching her breath from all her laughing. "But at least it's just a chocolate cake you're baking. You shouldn't run into any other trouble now that you've got the ingredients right."

"But it's not just a chocolate cake," he moaned.

"What do you mean?" Enid asked sharply.

"It's a raspberry-chocolate truffle cake," Todd lamented. "Making the cake batter is just the first step. I still have to make raspberry truffles to go in the middle of it," Todd explained in a voice full of despair.

"Ohhh . . ." Enid sighed sympathetically.

"And when I finish the cake, I was going to

make fo . . . foca . . ." Todd hesitated, not sure of his pronunciation.

"Focaccia?" Enid inquired. "As in, Italian bread?"

"Yeah, that's it," Todd answered. "I can't even pronounce it. I have no idea how I'm going to make it. . . ." His voice trailed off hopelessly. There was a long pause.

"Todd?" Enid said finally.

"Yeah?" he answered hopefully.

"Do you want me to come over and help you?" Enid asked compassionately.

Yes!

"That would be great, Enid," Todd gushed. "I'd really appreciate it. You don't know how much this means to me." Todd was so grateful, he wished he could hug her through the phone.

"You can thank me later," Enid said. "Maybe when this is all over, you and Liz can treat me to a lunch at the Dairi Burger."

"You bet!" Todd responded immediately. He knew he was in need of some serious help. "When can you be here?"

"I'll just make a quick stop at the grocery store, and I'll be right there," Enid said.

Todd hung up the phone and felt better instantly. "The cavalry is on its way!"

*   *   *

When Enid arrived, Todd greeted her promptly at the door. After a quick hello she marched straight into the kitchen and began emptying the contents of her grocery bags onto the counter. When she had finished, she looked around the room, noticing the mess for the first time.

"Oh, my gosh," she said, wide-eyed. "What happened in here?"

"I happened," Todd answered sheepishly.

"Wow, this is even worse than it sounded over the phone," Enid said, eyeing the ceiling, which had been splattered with chocolate during Todd's fiasco with the electric mixer. Enid wiped the grin off her face.

"OK, the first thing we need to do is clean this place up," she started authoritatively. "It's impossible to create anything in a messy kitchen." Todd stood stiffly and saluted her.

"Aye, aye, Captain," he said, clicking his heels together and executing a perfect military turn. Enid smirked.

"Ah, complete obedience," she joked. "I could get used to this."

Together the two of them managed to wipe up all the chocolate, flour, sugar, egg, and butter that Todd had spilled in his first attempt at cooking. It took them only about fifteen minutes to get the kitchen into shape, and then they were ready to proceed.

"What now, fearless leader?" Todd asked. He was glad Enid had come over. Just having the place clean again made him feel infinitely better.

"Now we start cooking," Enid said, walking over to the space where she had spread out the groceries. Todd moaned.

"This is the part I'm not so good at," he said, beginning to feel despondent once again.

"Don't worry," Enid consoled him. "I picked up some things to make it easier on you. Voilà!" She trailed her hand across the counter to call his attention to the various items she had brought with her.

"First we have a chocolate cake mix," she began.

"Isn't that cheating?" Todd protested. "I want to make sure Liz gets food that I've prepared with my own hands."

"I wasn't suggesting that you give her the box, Todd," Enid said sarcastically. "There's still plenty of preparation involved. Besides, you're not just making a chocolate cake. You're making a chocolate-raspberry trifle." Todd looked at her, confused.

"I'm pretty sure the recipe says *truffle*, Enid, not *trifle*," he said cautiously. Todd had decided that when it came to cooking, he wasn't completely sure of anything.

"Your recipe does say truffle," Enid agreed. "But I've decided you're making a *trifle* instead.

That's why I brought you a trifle bowl." She pointed to a glass container sitting on the counter. It was an elegant crystal bowl with a glass pedestal attached to the bottom. Todd narrowed his eyes and tilted his head to one side questioningly.

"What's the difference between a truffle and a trifle?" he asked. Enid observed his expression and laughed.

"Todd, with those big brown eyes and that confused face you look just like a puppy dog," she said. Todd's expression turned to a scowl.

"Just answer the question, Rollins," he directed her.

"Sorry," Enid apologized. "The difference is about two and a half hours and a lot less work," she explained. "With the truffle cake, you'd have to do all kinds of preparation in advance and you'd have to be really careful that the whole thing looked right when you were done. With a trifle you'll use approximately the same ingredients, but you'll crumble everything and layer it in this bowl. It will taste just as good, and it will be gorgeous no matter how bad you mess things up." Todd smiled. Getting Enid involved had definitely been a smart move.

"That's fantastic," he said with admiration. "What else have you got?" Enid grabbed a few more items from the counter.

"Raspberry preserves, which you can use for the filling. Whipped cream, which will save you the time of making your own, and mint leaves, which you can arrange around the top for extra flavor and garnishing all at once." Enid stood proudly holding the groceries. Todd was impressed, and he was even understanding how to put all of these things together now.

"So I just bake the cake, and then layer it alternately with the whipped cream and the raspberry stuff, and that's it?" he asked. Enid nodded. Todd was ecstatic. What had seemed impossible to him an hour ago now appeared to be an easy task.

"This is great," he said, on the verge of jumping up and down like a small child. Then he remembered the bread. "But what about the . . . foca . . . fo—"

"Focaccia," Enid said in an exaggeratedly slow voice.

"Yeah," Todd said. "What about that?"

Once again Enid gestured toward the items she had bought. She showed Todd that he could easily make the tasty Italian bread by starting with frozen bread dough instead of making his own. Basically all he had to do was spread it out in a pan, add fresh tomatoes, basil, garlic, and rosemary, and bake it.

"Jeez, Enid," Todd said appreciatively. "I don't know how to thank you enough. I actually feel like

I can handle this cooking thing easily now. I definitely owe you one."

"I think it's great that you're doing this for Elizabeth. I'm glad to help," she said warmly. "Elizabeth's lucky to have you. Most guys wouldn't go to this kind of trouble for their girlfriends. She's going to be so psyched." Todd was glad to have some words of encouragement.

"I hope you're right," he responded. There was a tiny bit of skepticism in his voice. "I've been spending so much time getting ready for the big surprise that I haven't seen much of her lately. And I'm going to need at least Friday night to finish the preparations." He remembered the nervous feeling that had come over him when he had walked into school that morning.

"It's weird," he added. "I'm even beginning to miss her."

"I'm sure it will all be worth it when you spring the big surprise on her," Enid reassured him. Todd was looking down at his feet distractedly. The strange nervous feeling had come back again.

"Don't worry about it," Enid added, clearly sensing his uneasiness. "You and Elizabeth are the most solid couple I know. Trust me, she's going to be ecstatic. Especially when she tastes your home-made creations."

Todd perked up.

"You're right," he said, grinning. "Who could resist the sumptuous creations of Chef Wilkins?"

Enid giggled. "So are you all set?" she asked, getting ready to leave.

"Absolutely," Todd assured her, walking her to the door. When they had reached the foyer, Enid stopped abruptly.

"Just one more thing," she said, turning to face Todd. "Those boxed cake mixes tend to be a little flat sometimes, so you might want to add an extra pinch of soda to help it rise."

"Wow, you know all the tricks," Todd said with respect. "I never would have thought of that. But what kind of soda should I use? Club soda or something like ginger ale?"

Enid's eyes widened and she shook her head, looking totally bewildered.

"What?" he asked defensively. "Did I say something wrong?"

"You're hopeless, Todd," Enid said, smiling. "That's *baking* soda. You know, the stuff you put in the freezer to keep it from getting all stinky." Enid and Todd exchanged concerned looks.

"Maybe I better stay," Enid suggested.

Todd didn't even hesitate. "I think that would be wise."

Chapter 8

Elizabeth closed her copy of *Macbeth* and set it down on the bed next to her. She had actually finished reading the play on Monday night, but Mr. Collins was going to discuss the final scenes in class tomorrow, so she had decided to reread the last act.

She took a deep breath and let it out slowly, contemplating the plot of the play and making sure she had it all straight in her head. Elizabeth knew a lot of her classmates despised studying Shakespeare, but she enjoyed it. On her fifteenth birthday her parents had given her a book containing all his plays and sonnets, and she had been an admirer of his work ever since. Her favorite sonnet was number eighteen, which began, "Shall I compare thee to a summer's day?"

Elizabeth closed her eyes and started to recite the rest of the poem to herself. Instantly she was reminded of Todd. Not too long ago he had gotten that sonnet printed on a tiny card for her and then made it into a bookmark. Elizabeth hopped off her bed and walked swiftly over to her desk. Sure enough, when she opened the top drawer, she saw the card lying there underneath an assortment of pens and pencils. She fished it out and read the entire sonnet silently. Then she flipped the narrow slip over and read Todd's inscription.

Dear Elizabeth,
    The words may be borrowed, but the sentiment is all mine.
                    With love,
                    Todd

As Elizabeth read his sweet words a wave of guilt swept over her. It suddenly occurred to her that she hadn't been spending much time with Todd lately. In fact, she didn't feel like she had seen him at all since last Saturday night, when they had gone to a movie together.

Elizabeth clutched the bookmark to her heart. *I'm a horrible girlfriend,* she told herself. *I've been so busy thinking about Devon that I haven't been paying any attention to Todd.*

How could she have been so insensitive? Elizabeth felt awful. *Poor Todd,* she thought. *He must be so upset with me.* Clearly she had to do something to remedy the situation right away.

She replaced the sonnet in her desk, shutting the top drawer, but then quickly changed her mind. Opening the drawer again, Elizabeth retrieved the card and tapped it lightly against her palm. *I should put this in a more prominent place,* she thought, biting her lower lip. *Maybe then I'll be reminded to keep my priorities straight.*

After a moment she tucked the bookmark between the rows of letters on her computer keyboard. That way she was certain to notice it every time she sat down at her desk. Satisfied, she turned and walked into the hallway to grab the cordless phone. Elizabeth had an extension in her room, but she preferred to use the remote telephone. That way she could move around freely while she was talking.

Thankfully, the phone was available. Snatching it from its cradle, Elizabeth returned to her room and dialed Todd's number. Then she sat down on her bed and waited. After only two rings Todd picked up.

"Wilkins residence," he said automatically.

"Wilkins residence?" Elizabeth repeated. "I must

have the wrong number. I was trying to order a pizza."

"Ha, ha, very funny, Liz," Todd returned dryly. "What's up?"

"I was going to ask you that very question," she said, drumming her fingers on her copy of *Macbeth.* "I feel like I haven't seen you in ages." Todd sighed heavily.

"That's funny," he remarked. "I was thinking the same thing earlier today."

As far as Elizabeth could tell, Todd wasn't angry at all. He *did* sound despondent, as though he missed her, but he didn't seem to think it was her fault that they hadn't seen each other. Elizabeth relaxed a little, feeling as though she had been let off the hook.

"Well, maybe we can do something about that," she replied more casually, leaning back on her pillow. "Do you want to see a movie or something on Friday night?"

To Elizabeth's surprise, there was a silence at the other end of the phone. She had expected Todd to jump at the chance to get together.

"Todd?" she asked. "Are you still there?"

"Oh, yeah . . . sorry . . . I was just . . . looking at the television and I got distracted," Todd answered falteringly. "What did you say?"

Elizabeth bit her lip. She hated talking on the phone when the person on the other end was preoccupied. It always made her feel like she was being ignored. She waited a moment and then spoke again.

"I just asked if you wanted to see a movie on Friday night," she repeated. Again Todd hesitated.

"A movie? Well, I suppose we could, but . . ." Todd's voice trailed off, leaving the thought unfinished. Elizabeth was beginning to get irritated with his lack of interest in the conversation.

Maybe he just doesn't feel like seeing a movie, she told herself. *After all, we did just go to one last weekend.*

"We could do something else," she offered. "Like dinner in town or ice cream at Casey's—or we could even just go for a drive," she suggested.

"I . . . uh . . . I can't," he stammered. "I have plans . . . with my family." Elizabeth wrinkled her nose. *Plans with his family? On a Friday night?* Not only did it seem odd that Todd would be spending a Friday night with his parents, but the response itself had sounded forced.

What's going on here? Elizabeth thought. *Why do I feel like he's feeding me a line?*

"Really?" she asked, not quite sure what to think. "What kind of plans?"

"Oh, nothing special," Todd said, speaking slowly. "We're just going to hang out. . . . You know, rent a movie or something. My parents have it in their heads that we don't spend enough time together as a family anymore, so they made me promise I'd spend Friday night at home with them."

Elizabeth was positively puzzled. *That doesn't sound like Mr. and Mrs. Wilkins at all,* she thought. *But then, why on earth would Todd make up something like that?*

Elizabeth tried to push her suspicious thoughts away, but she couldn't stop thinking that something strange was going on. It almost sounded as though Todd was concocting excuses not to go out with her.

Why would he do that? Elizabeth asked herself. *What possible reason could he have for not wanting to see me?* Her mind was reeling. She sat staring at the phone, not sure how to respond. Todd's strange behavior had rendered her speechless. Todd, on the other hand, was beginning to sound much more relaxed.

"I told my parents you'd understand," he continued, his voice steadier now. "You do understand, don't you, Liz?" Elizabeth was dumbfounded.

Understand? she steamed. *I understand that after not seeing me for a week, you're blowing me off, if that's what you mean.*

"Todd, I—," Elizabeth began, but she was interrupted by the familiar beep of call waiting in her ear. Normally Elizabeth didn't like to put anyone on hold in order to answer an incoming call, but tonight was an exception. She was so bewildered by Todd's apparent rejection that she welcomed the chance for a quick break. It would give her time to figure out how to respond to him.

"Can you hold on for a second, Todd?" she asked. "I have another call."

"Oh, sure," Todd answered quickly.

Hmph. He didn't have to think that *one over*, Elizabeth thought sarcastically as she switched to the other line.

"Hello?" she answered distractedly. She was still shaken from her unfinished discussion with Todd.

"Hello . . . Elizabeth?" the caller inquired. Elizabeth sat up straight on her bed, astonished by the familiar voice. *It can't be . . .* , she told herself, gripping the receiver tightly.

"Yes . . . this is Elizabeth," she replied tentatively.

"Hi," the voice answered. "It's Devon. I hope you don't mind me calling you at home." Elizabeth felt like her whole body had just been jump-started.

"Oh, no, not at all," she replied immediately, realizing that she was talking a mile a minute. *Get ahold of yourself, Elizabeth,* she thought. *It's just Devon.* She took a deep breath before speaking again.

"How are you?" she forced herself to ask more calmly.

"I'm fine," Devon answered. "Except for that spot on my hand where you spilled hydrochloric acid in chemistry class today. It's swollen to five times its natural size."

Elizabeth gasped, almost taking his bait, but then she caught herself.

"Yeah, right," she said doubtfully. "First of all, that hydrochloric acid was way too weak to be the least bit dangerous to human skin, and second, I spilled it on your arm, not your hand." Devon chuckled.

"Can't get anything past you, can I?" he teased. Elizabeth laughed too. She was glad Devon had called. He always managed to put her in a better mood.

"I just wanted to see what you were up to this Friday night," Devon said. "I thought maybe you'd be interested in having a study date."

Elizabeth's heart skipped a beat at the word *date*. She had already told Devon she couldn't go out with him. Was he asking her again?

"I'm not sure if—," Elizabeth started, but Devon cut her off.

"I thought we should go over the experiments we've done this week since Mr. Russo is planning to give us a quiz on Monday. What do you say? Can you spare some of your wisdom?"

Elizabeth thought it over. Mr. Russo *had* said there would be a quiz coming up and Devon *was* her lab partner, so it would be only natural to study with him. It seemed perfectly harmless. Besides, it wasn't like she had anything else to do on Friday night. *Todd's already confirmed that,* she reminded herself bitterly.

"I suppose I could attempt to share my vast knowledge of chemistry with you," she replied kiddingly. "That is, if it's not all over your head."

"I'll bring my dunce cap just in case," Devon shot back. They laughed easily together.

"So should I pick you up around seven?" Devon asked. Elizabeth almost agreed, but then she thought of Jessica. She didn't want her sister to see her leaving the house with Devon. She might think Elizabeth had a real date with him instead of just a study date, and if Jessica got the wrong idea . . .

"It would probably be better if I met you somewhere," she suggested.

"OK. How about the school parking lot?" Devon volunteered. "It's a central location, and it's one of the only places in Sweet Valley that I know how to find at this point."

"That sounds great," Elizabeth said. "So I'll see you then?"

"Yes," Devon answered. "But you'll see me in school tomorrow first."

"Oops! I guess I must be excited about cracking the books," she said sarcastically. "I forgot it's only Wednesday." Devon chuckled. "So I'll see you *tomorrow*," she said.

"Absolutely," Devon replied. "Unless I die in my sleep from that hydrochloric acid," he jested. Elizabeth sighed heavily.

"You're impossible," she said. "Bye, Devon."

"Bye," Devon replied.

Elizabeth shook her head and smiled to herself. Talking with Devon always made her feel better. She wasn't even terribly upset with Todd anymore. *Let him have his family night,* she thought. *It will be good to get some studying done early. Then I'll have the rest of my weekend free.*

Elizabeth was pleased with the way things had turned out. She switched back to the other line with a much improved attitude.

"Todd?" she asked.

"Right here," he answered quickly.

"So you were saying that you have plans with your parents for Friday night?" she asked.

"Yeah," Todd said. "I'm really sorry. But you know how parents can be."

"It's OK," Elizabeth reassured him. "I understand."

"You're the best, Liz," Todd gushed. "I'm so glad you're not upset with me. I was afraid you'd be mad since we haven't seen much of each other lately and everything."

"Not at all," Elizabeth confirmed. She felt foolish for having been so upset with him before. *I was ridiculous to think he was lying to me,* she told herself.

"You just have a good time and tell your parents I said hi. Maybe we can get together on Saturday or Sunday," Elizabeth suggested.

"That would be great," Todd answered enthusiastically. "Thanks again, Liz. You really are the greatest."

"Don't mention it," Elizabeth returned. "I'll talk to you soon."

"OK, bye," Todd said, sounding upbeat.

Elizabeth turned off the phone, pushed its antenna back down, and practically skipped into the hallway.

Things between her and Todd were fine, and she would be spending Friday night with Devon, which was sure to be fun. She always enjoyed talking with him, and he invariably seemed to be able to make her laugh, regardless of what kind of mood she was in.

As long as she could push aside her attraction to him for one night, she might even be able to get a lot of studying done.

*   *   *

If there was one thing Jessica Wakefield knew about guys, it was that they liked girls who showed an interest in stereotypical "guy" things—like sports, cars, and—motorcycles. As Jessica stood in the school parking lot Thursday morning and watched Devon pull in on his bike, she tried to wipe the self-satisfied smile from her face. Armed with the tons of research she had done on Elizabeth's computer, she was sure to have Devon kissing her feet before the first bell rang.

Normally Jessica wouldn't resort to these kinds of tactics. She usually didn't have to. Most guys flocked to her the second she flashed them her irresistible smile. But so far Devon hadn't responded to any of her usual ploys.

Drastic times call for drastic measures, she told herself. She smoothed her black leather miniskirt and adjusted the collar on her matching leather jacket. Jessica smiled devilishly to herself. *I'm even dressed for my role today,* she thought mischievously. *There's no way he'll be able to resist.*

Jessica marched confidently over to Devon and his bike, put one high-heeled boot up on a foot peg, and struck her most seductive pose. Devon was attaching his helmet to the rear of the bike and removing his leather satchel. He turned to face her and froze for a moment, staring. *This is it,* Jessica thought. *I've got him. He can't take his eyes off me.*

"This is a Sportster 1200 XLH, isn't it?" Jessica asked in a sultry voice. She knew perfectly well it was. She had been up half the night studying the different models of Harley-Davidson motorcycles and quizzing herself. Devon leaned closer to her and continued to stare.

Jessica was on fire inside. She was mentally congratulating herself on her brilliant scheme when suddenly Devon asked her a strange question.

"Did you have a bagel for breakfast?" he inquired. Jessica blinked.

"Yes," she answered, caught completely off guard.

"I thought so. You've got a piece of raisin stuck on your tooth," he said, pointing. "Right there."

Jessica was mortified. Was that what he had been focused on? Her teeth? How could he possibly notice her teeth when she was wearing this sexy outfit and talking about motorcycles? She turned her head and scratched at her tooth quickly, but she didn't feel anything. Meanwhile Devon had started to walk toward the school.

"You better hurry," he called over his shoulder. "You don't want to be late for your first class."

"Devon!" she shouted after him. "What about the bike?" He turned around, walking backward.

"Yes," he called back to her. "It's a Sportster.

126

Feel free to look it over if you want." With that he turned and entered the building. Jessica was furious.

This cannot be happening, she told herself.

How could he ignore her like that? She had never had this much trouble getting a guy's attention before. Regardless of what she tried, Devon remained politely distant. And ironically, the more distant he acted, the more irresistible Jessica found him.

This isn't over, Devon, she thought. *You can play cool all you want, but sooner or later you're going to have to give in.*

Getting Devon to go out with her had become more than a desire—it had become a challenge. And it was one Jessica did not intend to let go.

Chapter 9

"Thanks, Bill," Todd said, patting his friend on the back. "I'm going to need all the help I can get."

He and Bill Chase were making their way through the line in the cafeteria at lunchtime. Todd had asked Bill to help him cart everything he needed for his celebration with Elizabeth out to the beach on Monday.

"No problem," Bill answered. "The surf-mobile is at your service."

Not too long ago Bill had won the state surfing championship, and ever since, the van he carried his gear in had been known as his "surf-mobile." In fact, Bill himself had become synonymous with surfing as far as the students of Sweet Valley High were concerned. And with his light blond hair, bright blue eyes, and dark tan, he definitely looked the part.

"So exactly what do you have planned?" he asked Todd as they both grabbed trays and began sliding them along the steel counter. A bright smile crossed Todd's face as he started to explain.

"First I'm going to set up my radio on the beach so that when Elizabeth arrives, she'll hear some of her favorite tunes playing softly in the background," he said proudly.

"What did you do, buy a radio station for her?" Bill joked.

"No," Todd answered with a laugh. "Maria Slater is putting together some music for me. She makes all the cheerleaders' tapes, so she has access to some really good equipment and a lot of songs."

"Wow, you've really planned ahead for this," Bill said, nodding and looking at Todd with admiration.

"Yeah, but that's not all," Todd continued. "I'm also going to treat her to a sampling of her favorite foods, prepared by none other than the famous cook Chef Wilkins."

Bill had just grabbed an apple from the fruit cart and was about to bite into it, but he stopped at Todd's words.

"You're actually *cooking?*" he asked with a look of sheer disbelief. "I didn't know you could cook."

"I couldn't until yesterday," Todd responded with a short laugh. "Enid came over and gave me

129

some quick tips." Bill was clearly impressed.

"So now you're a gourmet chef?" he asked kiddingly. Todd squinted and thought it over.

"Sort of," he answered tentatively. "More like a gourmet in training. Enid's going to supervise me while I bake to make sure I don't mess anything up."

"Hey, just being able to turn on the oven makes you a more qualified cook than I am," Bill joked. "I can't even make instant soup without burning the water."

Todd laughed and continued to move through the lunch line. He grabbed a container of milk and an ice cream sandwich from the freezer compartment and then moved to the cash register to pay.

"Do you have any other tricks up your sleeve?" Bill asked as he and Todd walked over to an unoccupied table in the back. Todd slid into a seat and leaned forward conspiratorially.

"Jessica's going to the mall with me after school tomorrow to help me pick out a special gift for Liz," Todd explained, pausing to take a big bite out of his turkey sandwich. "But I've already got one part of it all set."

"Well," Bill goaded, "are you going to let me in on it?"

"Calm down," Todd replied. "I'm getting to it." He took a sip of his milk and then looked back at

Bill. "I asked Mr. Collins to get me a copy of Elizabeth's article—the first one she had published—and I had it framed for her. It looks great."

"That's a fantastic idea," Bill said after swallowing a bite of pizza. "Elizabeth is going to flip when she sees all the trouble you've gone to." Todd bit the inside of his cheek.

"I sure hope so," he said uncertainly.

"What do you mean by that?" Bill asked, puzzled. "Of course she will. Why wouldn't she?"

"I don't know," he said slowly. "It's just that . . . I have a weird nervous feeling about the whole thing." Bill's eyebrows shot up in surprise.

"Well, when was the last time you talked to her?" he asked.

"I talked to her on the phone last night," Todd said. "And I saw her between classes yesterday . . . but I haven't really had much time to spend with her lately. I've been so busy planning this surprise that—"

"There's your problem," Bill interrupted. "People in relationships always let their fears run away with them when they've been apart for a while."

"Do you really think so?" Todd asked.

"Sure," Bill replied confidently. "It's just like a long-distance relationship. When you can't see your girlfriend every day, you start to worry that maybe she's seeing someone else or she doesn't like you anymore. You know, stupid stuff like that."

Bill's theory made sense. It was possible that he was just imagining things since he hadn't seen Elizabeth much lately.

"Maybe you're right," he conceded.

Bill slapped the table dramatically and stood up. "Of course I'm right," he declared. "So stop your worrying." Todd smiled, feeling better.

"I'm going to grab one of those ice cream sandwiches," Bill said, pointing at the one Todd was eating. "Do you want anything?" Todd shook his head, and Bill walked back up to the lunch line.

In another four days Elizabeth and I will be sitting on the beach celebrating her big day, and everything will feel right again, Todd thought.

He smiled to himself, comforted by the thought of things returning to normal. The romantic night he and Liz were going to share on Monday would be worth all the time he'd put into planning it.

In fact, he was sure that he and Elizabeth would be enjoying romantic nights for years to come.

Devon walked out of his calculus class and headed straight for his locker. As far as he was concerned, the day hadn't gone fast enough. Once chemistry class with Elizabeth was over, he had wanted the rest of the day to fly by. He had some important errands to run after school, and he hadn't been able to think about anything else.

Elizabeth's going to be so surprised, he thought as he sped past the other students and turned left into the junior corridor. Even though their study date wasn't until tomorrow night, Devon had a few things he needed to prepare in advance. *A few things that will make her head spin,* he told himself, barely able to contain his excitement.

Devon was aware of the wide grin on his face and knew he must look ridiculously happy, but he didn't care. Elizabeth had finally agreed to go out with him, even if it was just a study date, and nothing could have pleased him more.

He quickened his steps, eager to get started on his preparations for tomorrow night, but then something caught his eye that almost brought him to a standstill. Jessica was standing next to his locker, and he was certain that she was waiting for him. *Now there's one girl who just won't give up,* Devon thought, proceeding more slowly. He saw Jessica straighten up and smile in his direction, and he knew he had been spotted.

"Hi, Devon," she called when he was within hearing range.

"So how are you, Jessica?" he asked flatly, turning his attention to his lock. Out of the corner of his eye he could see that Jessica was twirling her hair around one finger and staring at him.

"I'm fabulous," she responded, moving closer so it was harder for Devon to avoid looking at her. "But I'm actually in kind of a hurry. I have to get to cheerleading practice." She was practically standing in front of him now. Reluctantly Devon gave in and turned his head toward her.

"They can barely get anything done without me," she continued, looking straight into Devon's eyes. "I'm one of the cocaptains, you know." Jessica tilted her head to one side and flipped back her hair.

"So I've heard," Devon returned. "Well, don't be late on my account." Jessica crinkled her nose flirtatiously.

"I don't mind," she told him, smiling slyly. Then she straightened up again and her expression turned more sober. "But I do have an important matter to discuss with you."

"And what might that be?" Devon asked. If it was serious, maybe it had something to do with Elizabeth. The playful smile returned to Jessica's face.

"I wanted to invite you to an exclusive soiree at Bruce Patman's house tomorrow night," she said excitedly. "It would be a great opportunity for you to meet people. Strictly A-list," she added in a low whisper.

Am I supposed to be impressed? Devon wondered cynically. But Jessica looked so excited that he knew he couldn't possibly share his thought aloud. He didn't want to hurt her feelings.

"Have I met Bruce?" Devon asked instead.

"I don't know," Jessica answered. "He's a senior and he's kind of a snob, but he throws the most amazing parties."

Devon forced a smile onto his face. "We'll see," he said. "I'll try to make it." It didn't sound like his scene, but he didn't want to shoot her down completely.

"Try really hard," she said coyly, batting her lashes at him. Then she flashed him one last smile and started down the hallway. When she was only three steps away, she turned back to him.

"Oh, I almost forgot. It starts at eight o'clock, and I wrote down the directions so you could find it easily." Jessica handed him a slip of paper. "My phone number is at the bottom of the sheet if you have any questions," she added with a sly look. "I'll be arriving at eight myself, so you don't have to worry about being left in a roomful of strangers. And I'll introduce you to everybody. Trust me, it'll be a great time," she promised. Then she turned and bounded down the corridor.

Yeah, I bet, Devon thought sarcastically, stuffing the slip of paper into his pocket. He turned back to his locker and fumbled with the lock again. *Jessica can go to her party and enjoy all her A-list friends, but I've got bigger and better plans,* he thought, beaming. *I'm going to have a study date that will knock Elizabeth Wakefield's socks off.*

"What do you think of this one?" Jessica asked, holding up an extravagant gold pin encrusted with several small diamonds. Todd flashed her a disapproving look.

"Why do I have the feeling that if I bought that for Elizabeth, it would end up in your jewelry box instead of hers?" he questioned her.

"So what's wrong with that?" she asked playfully. Todd continued to scowl at her until she gave in.

"Oh, all right," she said reluctantly, replacing the pin in its case. "It's probably too flashy for Liz. But let's not get anything too boring."

"I'll try not to disappoint you," Todd responded with a laugh. He and Jessica were at North's Jewelry Store in the Valley Mall looking for a present for Elizabeth. They had been shopping for about an hour now but couldn't agree on anything.

All the items Jessica picked out were clearly more appropriate for her than for Elizabeth. And every time Todd showed Jessica something he liked, she just turned up her nose and said something along the lines of, "It's all right . . . if you're shopping for your mother."

Todd was beginning to feel like they'd never find something they both thought Elizabeth would appreciate. In fact, he was on the verge of thanking Jessica for her help and telling her he'd come back by himself to find something tomorrow. But even though Jessica was a pain to shop with, Todd was aware that no one knew Elizabeth's taste better than she did. He just had to get her focused on the task at hand.

Suddenly Todd spotted something he thought would be perfect. He called Jessica over and pointed into the glass jewelry case.

"What do you think about that?" he asked.

Todd had singled out a sterling silver ring that was shaped like two tiny pencils coming together. In the center, where the points met, there was a small diamond of about a quarter carat. It sparkled brilliantly in the fluorescent lighting. Todd thought it was exquisite.

"It's definitely unique," Jessica began. Todd noticed that her tone was bordering on approval. "And it certainly suits the occasion." Jessica seemed to be choosing her words carefully, but Todd could tell that she liked it. He opened the case, which the clerk had unlocked for him earlier, and removed the ring. Jessica took it from him and

137

slid it on her finger. Todd watched her cautiously. He wanted to make sure she remembered she wasn't shopping for herself.

"Don't forget," Todd told her, "this is for Liz."

"I know," Jessica said, rolling her eyes. "Like I would ever want a ring with pencils on it. But I do happen to resemble my sister. Don't you want to see what it would look like on her?" she asked, holding out her hand.

He looked at the ring on Jessica's finger. It was fabulous. The smooth silver glistened brightly, and the sparkling diamond was the crowning touch. He was positive Elizabeth would adore it. All he needed now was Jessica's approval. She wiggled her fingers, examining the ring from several different angles. Finally she smiled at Todd.

"This is nice," Jessica said sincerely. "I think Liz will like it." Then she took off the ring and turned over the price tag so she could read it. Her eyes widened.

"Wow!" she said, obviously more impressed by the price than by the ring itself. "Did you look at this yet?"

"Yeah," Todd answered, downplaying the expense. "That's about what I expected to spend." Jessica stared at him, surprised.

"Jeez, I'm going to tell my sister to hold on to you," she joked.

"Thanks, Jess," Todd said wryly. "So do you really think she'll like it?"

"Of course she will," Jessica answered confidently. "And you don't have to worry. I think it's nice, but it's not quite my style, so I probably won't be stealing it from Liz's room. At least not permanently," she quipped. Todd chuckled.

"That's good to hear," he said with a smile.

"It's absolutely perfect, and I don't think we could do better even if we did spend the whole night looking," Jessica reassured him.

Todd grinned. He felt better hearing it put that way. "Great," he said. "I'll get the clerk so I can pay for it and have it boxed."

Todd chose silver gift wrap and watched closely as the salesclerk wrapped the ring box and placed a big matching bow on top.

"So you have a plan to get Liz to the beach on Monday, right?" he asked Jessica as they walked over to the cash register.

"Everything is all set," Jessica answered. "Elizabeth thinks we're having a sisters' night out, and she's meeting me by her locker right after school on Monday."

"You're sure?" Todd asked.

"Yes," Jessica said. She was beginning to sound annoyed. "Calm down, already. She'll be at the beach at four o'clock exactly." Todd knew he was

being overbearing but couldn't seem to help himself. The more time he spent planning Elizabeth's
special evening, the more important it was becoming to him.

"Sorry, Jess," he apologized. "It's just that I've
put a lot of work into this night. I know I keep
bugging you about it, but I really want everything
to be—"

"Perfect?" Jessica asked. Todd laughed. She
had certainly nailed him on that one.

"Exactly," he said.

Chapter 10

"Can I take this thing off now?" Elizabeth asked, tugging at the strip of cloth covering her eyes.

"In one minute," Devon answered quickly, batting down her hand.

Elizabeth was sitting at the edge of the softball field in back of Sweet Valley High with Devon. She could hear him scurrying around arranging something, but she had no idea what he was up to.

She had met him in the school parking lot at seven o'clock for their study date, just as they had arranged. Elizabeth had suggested they go to L'Autre Chose, a coffee bar near the mall, to study, and Devon had agreed. But then he had told her he had something important to show her first. Another one of his minichemistry lessons. Elizabeth was immediately intrigued. She was always up for another demonstration of Devon's incredible knack for science.

"Come on, Devon!" Elizabeth prodded. She could feel her heart pounding in anticipation.

"Just one more minute," Devon said gleefully.

What could he possibly have planned? she kept asking herself excitedly. After all the experiments they had done in class and all the gifts he had made for her, she knew it would be wonderful. Devon never did anything halfway.

Suddenly she felt Devon's hands at the back of her head.

"Are you ready?" he asked, untying the blindfold.

"Absolutely," Elizabeth answered. "This better be good, Whitelaw."

"OK. Open your eyes," he instructed.

Elizabeth blinked a few times and looked around. At first she didn't see anything, but, of course, it was getting dark outside, and she had no idea what she should be looking for. Then, all of a sudden, she saw an explosion in the air in front of her.

Devon was making her see fireworks—literally.

At first they came slowly, loud booms followed by brilliant displays of colors. Then everything sped up. The fireworks came quickly, one after another, earsplitting pops crackling in the air. Red, blue, violet, green. It was absolutely dazzling.

Elizabeth stared in astonishment, blown away by yet another fabulous chemistry lesson courtesy of Devon. She knew the fireworks were illegal, but she didn't care. It only added to the appeal of the whole night. This was certainly the best study date she had ever had.

Devon stood beside her, grinning like a kid on Christmas morning.

"I wanted to have the *1812 Overture* by Tchaikovsky playing in the background, but I couldn't get a radio down here with all of the other stuff I had to carry," he explained.

"I love that piece," Elizabeth said, humming the first few notes. Devon joined in, and they continued together through laughter. They finished their tune in perfect time with the grand finale of the fireworks display. When it was done, Elizabeth turned to Devon, her face glowing.

"That was incredible—," she started, but she was cut off by one last firework exploding. The sudden crack was unexpected, and Elizabeth jumped, grabbing Devon's arm. Now as she turned back to face him, she found he was only inches away.

She gazed into his intense blue eyes, and he looked at her through his thick, dark lashes. Elizabeth felt her heart pounding. She had been dazzled, all right, and not just by the fireworks. She could feel the amazing attraction between her and Devon growing stronger by the second.

He was so incredible. Everything about him excited her. His intelligence, his sense of humor, his ability to open her mind to new things, his gorgeous looks. More than anything she wanted to collapse into him and feel his arms around her.

"Come on, Elizabeth," he whispered, his voice husky. His lips were just inches from hers, and she could feel his warm, sweet breath on her cheek. "Admit it. You feel the connection between us just as much as I do."

Elizabeth's body swayed. "But I have a boyfriend," she whispered weakly, unable to tear her eyes away from his.

"Then why are you here with me?" he asked, moving closer almost imperceptibly.

Elizabeth didn't have an answer for that one. She had convinced herself that this night would be innocent, but it was rapidly becoming anything but that.

"What . . . what about Jessica?" Elizabeth asked desperately.

"What about her?" Devon breathed. "She's just as beautiful as you are . . ."

Elizabeth's eyes widened. She felt a momentary pinch of hurt.

"But she's not you," he finished. "And I'm not Todd."

Their foreheads were touching now. Elizabeth's breath quickened. If she moved an inch, their lips would touch and then she'd be a goner for sure.

Elizabeth knew she should turn away, but she couldn't. She didn't want to look away from Devon at all. She opened her mouth slightly, trying to find something to say, but Devon stopped her. "Don't say anything right now," he said softly. "Just think about it."

Elizabeth's mind was swimming in a murky haze as she tried to focus on his words.

"Think about going on a date with me—a real date," he added. "I want our relationship to move beyond chemistry class."

"But . . . but Todd—," Elizabeth started to protest. Devon touched his index finger to her lips, and a jolt of electricity shot through Elizabeth.

"People change and they move on," Devon said quietly. "That's what you need to do. I know you don't want to hurt Todd. Neither do I. But you have to do what's right for *you*. You can't make all your decisions based on how they'll make other people feel."

He put his hand on Elizabeth's chin and cradled her head gently. "You and Todd don't belong together anymore," he said, looking deep into her eyes. "You belong with me, Elizabeth. I knew it the first moment I saw you."

Elizabeth recognized the heat of his touch on her face. She could feel the electricity between them surging throughout her body.

"I'll be at the Box Tree Café tomorrow night at eight o'clock, and I'll be waiting for you," he said finally. "I hope you'll come."

With that, Devon stood up and moved away from Elizabeth. She watched as he gathered the supplies he had brought down with him in a duffel bag and made his way back up the trail. When he was out of sight, she exhaled sharply and lay back on the ground.

She was still breathless from having been so close to him. She took several deep breaths and tried to calm herself down, but she could still feel the touch of his hand on her chin—his breath on her face.

Elizabeth touched the spot on her chin where Devon's hand had been and took another deep breath. She knew she had a tough decision ahead of her.

"So where's Devon?" Lila asked, taking a sip of her sparkling cider.

"He'll be here," Jessica answered moodily. She glanced at the antique grandfather clock

146

against the wall. *Eight forty-five,* she noted. *He better get here soon. I've had just about enough of his cool act.*

She dipped her potato chip in the crystal bowl of sour cream and chives on Bruce's elegant dining-room table and shoved it in her mouth.

"Hungry, Jess?" Lila asked with an amused smirk.

"What's that supposed to mean?" Jessica shot back as she munched.

"Just that you've been hanging out at the food table for the last half hour stuffing your face," Lila answered. "You wouldn't be trying to keep an eye on the front door for your precious biker man, would you?"

"Biker man?" Amy Sutton turned from the conversation she was having with Maria Santelli.

Great, Jessica thought. She really needed everyone involved in her dissed misery.

"Maybe he's lost," Lila said archly.

"What biker man?" Amy asked, tucking a strand of ash blond hair behind her ear. Amy was always eager for gossip. "Are you talking about the new guy? Is he supposed to be here tonight?"

"Jessica invited him," Lila offered. Jessica shot her best friend a scathing look. It was so obvious she was trying to embarrass her.

"Jessica?" Amy gasped. "Are you being stood up?"

147

"Hardly," Jessica answered. "Devon just knows how to be fashionably late."

He should be here by now, she thought, annoyed. *My directions were perfect. What's he waiting for?* Jessica was getting upset. She hated to be kept waiting, especially when she had gone to such great lengths herself to arrive on time.

Jessica had reasoned that the earlier she got to the party, the more time she would have with Devon. And the longer he had to see her mingling with all her friends, the sooner he was certain to fall head over heels in love with her. After all, who could possibly resist her when she was the life of the party?

But things hadn't gone exactly as she had planned. She *was* surrounded by friends, but instead of worshiping her for snagging the hottest guy in school, they were totally mocking her.

"Have you tried the caviar, Jessica?" Heather Malone had just walked over and squeezed her way into the conversation. "It's so fabulous—it just might take your mind off the fact that you're dateless." Heather was the cocaptain of the cheerleading squad and Jessica's fiercest rival. The curly-haired ice princess was the last person Jessica wanted to be clued in on her current miserable state. She watched with a sneer as Heather spread a generous helping of caviar onto a cracker.

148

"That stuff is disgusting," Jessica commented. "I don't know how you can eat it."

Heather looked straight at Jessica and took a bite of her hors d'oeuvre. Then, dabbing at the corners of her mouth with a napkin, she pressed her lips together in a smug smile.

"It's an acquired taste," she explained, lifting her head arrogantly. "You really should try some. It's a favorite with the upper echelon."

Rather than answer Heather's idiotic attempt at an insult, Jessica rolled her eyes and glanced over at the door again, hoping to see Devon enter.

"Poor Jessica," Heather murmured. "She's so upset about being stood up, she can't even think of a comeback."

"I am not being stood up," Jessica insisted, placing her hands on her hips. She was irritated by the fact that her audience seemed to be growing. Maria and her boyfriend, Winston, had joined Heather, Amy, and Lila now and were watching her with amused smiles.

"It's not an official date, and I'm not even sure if he can come," Jessica continued lamely. "He said he'd try to make it, but he thought he might have to do something at home."

"Like what?" Amy giggled. "Wash his hair?" Jessica groaned and shot Amy a dirty look. She was about to tell them all off when she heard the front door open. She spun around, knowing it had to be Devon. But her spirits fell when she saw Jeffrey French and Aaron Dallas walk in carrying bags of food.

"Calm down, Jess!" Lila laughed. "You don't want to pounce on innocent boys."

Everyone laughed, and Jessica felt an angry blush rising to her cheeks.

"Hey, everyone, back off!" Winston said. "I know Devon, and he's not the type to just stand someone up."

"Maybe Jessica's just the type that gets stood up," Heather said, prompting another round of giggles.

Jessica glared at her friends. She had had just about enough of this. It was bad enough that Devon had left her hanging—again. She didn't need her so-called friends rubbing it in her face. She folded her arms across her chest and opened her mouth to give them all a piece of her mind, but this time she was interrupted by a male voice from behind.

"What's going on over here?" Bruce asked, putting his hands on Jessica's shoulders and making her cringe. Bruce might throw good parties, but he didn't exactly have a special place in Jessica's heart. In fact, she pretty much detested the guy and avoided him completely unless there was something she could get out of him. "I know the spread is awesome, but it's not a good sign when half the party is gathering at the food table instead of mingling."

"Oh, don't worry, Bruce," Lila began with a jaunty look in her eyes. "We're just comforting Jessica because—"

"Because you haven't asked me to dance yet," Jessica interrupted. There was no way Jessica was going to let Lila tell Bruce about Devon too. He would never let her live it down. She turned to face Bruce and looked up at him coquettishly. Bruce smiled widely, revealing his perfectly straight, pearly white teeth. His smug smile made Jessica want to puke all over his newly shined shoes, but she forced herself to smile back.

"You'll have to forgive me for taking so long, Jessica," he said snidely. "So many girls, so little time, you know."

Give me a break, Jessica thought.

"Fortunately this is a situation we can remedy immediately," Bruce said, taking her hand. "Would you care to dance?"

Jessica batted her eyelashes at him exaggeratedly and clutched her heart with her free hand.

"I thought you'd never ask," she said sarcastically—a tone that was lost on Bruce's thick head. As she allowed him to lead her to the dance floor

Jessica looked back over her shoulder, shooting Lila a cold look to let her know that their conversation wasn't finished.

The crowd on the dance floor parted to allow the host and his partner into the middle. Jessica was pleased to be back at the center of the attention, where she belonged, but she was still upset with Devon. She danced with Bruce, smiling as though she was having the time of her life, but the thoughts inside her head were of a completely different nature.

Devon Whitelaw, you better have a good excuse for missing this party. If you don't, you're going to be sorry you ever met me.

What am I going to do? Elizabeth thought hopelessly.

She was lying on her bed, flipping through old photo albums. It seemed like the majority of her most memorable moments were connected in some way to Todd. There were numerous pictures of him throughout the album. As Elizabeth flipped the pages she was reminded of all the fun things they had done together.

There was a picture of Todd on the motorcycle he had owned for a short time. That bike had meant a lot to him, but he had been willing to sell it simply because Elizabeth wasn't comfortable riding on it with him.

Another picture showed the two of them arm in arm, dressed up for a formal dance at the school. Todd was wearing a tux, and Elizabeth had on a gorgeous black beaded gown with long, elegant matching gloves. She remembered how nervous Todd had been when the time came for him to pin on her corsage. His hands were shaking so much that he kept sticking himself with the pin. It was the first time they had ever gone to a black-tie event together.

Elizabeth recalled all the memories with fondness. But regardless of how much she tried to concentrate on Todd, she knew it was Devon who really occupied her thoughts. She couldn't believe how much her feelings had changed since she had met Devon.

How could I have been so completely in love with Todd just a week ago and feel so far away from him now? she asked herself. *And why does Devon have to be so wonderful? So perfect?*

Just as a single tear fell to the plastic surface of the photo album and splattered, Jessica burst into her room.

"You wouldn't *believe* what happened to me tonight!" Jessica cried wildly. Elizabeth looked up at her twin, wiping at her eyes with the back of her hand.

"What's the matter, Jess?" Elizabeth asked,

concerned, trying to hide her melancholy mood.

"Apparently our Mr. Whitelaw would rather spend his Friday night studying than going to a party." Jessica was fuming. She stomped across the room and sat down heavily on the pale velvet chaise lounge. Elizabeth jumped at the mention of Devon's name.

"What do you mean?" Elizabeth asked, slightly alarmed. Jessica couldn't possibly know about her study date with Devon this evening—could she?

"I could just kill him," Jessica ranted. "I went out of my way to invite him to an *exclusive* gathering at Bruce's house tonight—I'm talking about a party that could have ensured his acceptance by all the hippest people in Sweet Valley—and he didn't show! Can you believe the nerve?" Jessica stared at her twin incredulously, her eyes savage and her jaw slack.

Elizabeth allowed herself a short sigh of relief, but she wasn't home free yet.

"Do you have any idea what he did instead?" she asked innocently, trying to appear disinterested in the whole issue.

Jessica shook her head. "How am I supposed to know?" she shot back at her sister. "He just better have a good excuse. That's all I can say. If I find out he skipped the party to stay home and watch TV or study or something, I'll just . . . I'll just—"

"Calm down, Jessica," Elizabeth said quickly. She couldn't remember the last time she'd seen her sister so incensed. *She must really like Devon,* Elizabeth thought. But who could blame the girl? "Devon's very responsible. I'm sure he had a good reason for not going to Bruce's party."

Elizabeth had to struggle to keep from smiling at the irony of her own statement. *I just hope he comes up with an excuse by Monday morning, or he's going to have to deal with the wrath of Jessica.*

"Responsible, huh?" Jessica said, narrowing her eyes. She sat up straighter and peered at Elizabeth. "You sure seem to know a lot about Devon. Is there something you're not telling me?"

Elizabeth swallowed hard, her heart thumping. Had Jessica already seen right through her? "Like what?" Elizabeth managed.

"Like, did you ever get a chance to talk to Devon for me?" Elizabeth let out a long breath. How was she supposed to answer that? She *had* talked to Devon about Jessica, but she hadn't gotten the results her sister was hoping for. Not remotely.

I can't possibly tell her that Devon isn't interested in her because of me, Elizabeth thought. *She'd never forgive me.* She thought about the fireworks display Devon had put on for her and how he had said she needed to forget about Todd and move on. *But if I do plan to start seeing Devon, I'm going to have to tell her about it sooner or later.*

Elizabeth felt like she was in a no-win situation. What was she going to do? Was she actually going to leave Todd for Devon? And if so, what would she tell Jessica?

Elizabeth looked from her sister down to the photo of Todd in his tuxedo. His large brown eyes stared up at her. He looked so sweet, so loyal. So trusting. *How can I possibly hurt him?* she thought. *Or Jessica?*

"Liz?" Jessica asked again, obviously waiting for an answer. In a split second Elizabeth made a decision. She forced herself to speak before she could change her mind.

"I talked to him today," Elizabeth answered. "He mentioned that he was going to be at the Box Tree Café tomorrow night—alone. I think you should probably stop by. I have a hunch he'll be wanting some company."

Jessica's face lit up. "I see," she said, a wide smile replacing her formerly distraught features. "He wants to see me *alone*. No wonder he didn't come to the party." She jumped up from the divan, snapping back to life in true Jessica style.

"This is fantastic!" she squealed, running over to Elizabeth and giving her a big hug. "I knew you'd come through for me, sis!"

Elizabeth watched in misery as her sister danced around the room, ecstatic.

"You'll have to come into my room later and help me pick out something fabulous to wear," Jessica said anxiously. "Or maybe I'll just go to the mall tomorrow and buy something new," she decided, hugging Elizabeth once again. "Thanks so much, Lizzie. You really are super. I'm going to go call Lila and tell her the great news." Jessica ran out of the room, slamming the door behind her.

Elizabeth sat in the middle of her bed, feeling like she had just been run over by a steamroller. She couldn't believe what she had just done. She had given up her chance to be with Devon, the most exciting and wonderful guy she had ever met. But she had no other choice, did she?

I did the right thing, she told herself. *I know I did.* Maybe if she repeated it enough, she would begin to believe it herself.

Chapter 11

Jessica stepped from the Jeep in one graceful motion. She readjusted her outfit and glanced quickly at her face in the side mirror. Pressing her lips together and shaking back her hair, she observed her image.

"Perfect. I certainly hope Devon's prepared for me," she mused, strutting across the parking lot.

Jessica was dressed to kill. She wore a snug-fitting black minidress with thin shoulder straps. Though she had wanted to wear black platform shoes to emphasize the length of her tanned legs, she had decided against it. She reasoned that she and Devon might go for a stroll on the beach, and sandals would be a better choice.

After long hours in front of the mirror Jessica had finally decided to let her silky blond hair hang loosely around her shoulders. She had tried putting it up to look more elegant, but it didn't seem right. Wearing it down made her look more carefree, like she belonged at the beach.

Jessica climbed the small staircase that led to the deck where the café's outdoor tables were. As soon as she got to the top Jessica spotted Devon sitting alone in a secluded corner.

Jessica straightened up and tried to calm the fluttering in her heart. She sauntered over to him the way a model would walk on a runway in a fashion show. When Devon noticed her approaching, he immediately stood up, a grin lighting his face.

He's actually happy to see me for a change, Jessica thought.

"Hi, Devon," she said huskily.

"Hi, yourself," Devon returned with just a hint of seduction.

He put his arms around her and pulled her close. Jessica was in sheer bliss.

She returned the embrace, wrapping her arms around his neck. She smelled a hint of cologne on his neck and inhaled deeply. It was a perfect scent for him. Not too strong or fragrant, just clean, fresh, and masculine. Jessica savored the moment, taking in every detail. His soft hair brushing against her cheek, the noise of his leather jacket as he moved, the soft fabric of his T-shirt. It was all

159

just as she had imagined it would be. Her night with Devon was finally here.

"I knew you'd come, Elizabeth," he breathed into her ear, still holding her tight. "I knew you couldn't stay away."

Jessica stiffened.

Elizabeth! Why on earth would he think I'm Elizabeth? she thought. *What's going on here?* Jessica pulled away from him and looked at him in confusion.

Suddenly Devon looked puzzled. Jessica could see that he was beginning to question which Wakefield sister was actually standing before him. A fierce anger welled up inside her, surrounded by a crushing disappointment.

So he really was expecting Liz, she thought resentfully as her heart broke wide open. Jessica realized Devon didn't want her at all. It was her sister he had fallen for. And it was Elizabeth who he had intended to meet here. At first she wasn't sure how to respond, but one thing was for certain. There was no way she was going to let Devon Whitelaw see how he had affected her.

Without missing a beat Jessica launched into her best Elizabeth imitation, squelching the tumultuous emotions inside her. She backed away from Devon a little and began to adjust her outfit, tugging the hem of her dress down lower on her legs.

160

Then she pushed her hair back behind her ears nervously.

"I'm sorry I pulled away from you," she said in tones that echoed Elizabeth's manner of speaking perfectly. "I'm just a little nervous about being here." The warm smile returned to Devon's face, and Jessica knew instantly that she had him fooled. He moved closer to her again and took her hand tenderly.

"That's understandable," he said, his voice gentle and sincere. "But don't worry. Everything is going to be fine. I'm just glad you showed up here tonight. It shows that you can't ignore what's happening between us any more than I can."

Jessica couldn't believe her ears. *Exactly what is going on between you and my sister? That's what I'd like to know,* she thought angrily, hoping she wouldn't cry. Devon was the first guy Jessica had cared about in ages. She thought that tonight she would get to know him and make him fall head over heels for her. Instead she was slowly realizing she'd been betrayed by her sister in the worst way. *How could you do this to me, Liz? One perfect boyfriend isn't enough, so you needed to take mine too?*

Devon paused and looked deeply into Jessica's eyes. He touched her right cheek lightly with the back of his hand, tracing the line of her cheekbone

161

and tucking a stray piece of hair behind her ear.

"Let's just relax and have a good time tonight," he said. "Then we'll figure out what to do next."

Next? Jessica fumed, struggling to keep the smile plastered on her face. *Just how far is Elizabeth planning on taking this little affair?*

As Jessica slid into her seat she grabbed her water glass and took a sip, trying to mask her confusion and anger.

Devon was obviously relieved to see her relaxing a little. He held her hand in his and spoke to her in a quiet but husky voice.

"You won't be sorry that you came," he promised.

No, Jessica thought. *My back-stabbing sister's the one who's going to be sorry.*

As Elizabeth walked up the pathway to the Wilkinses' front doorstep she felt positively miserable. She hadn't been able to get Devon out of her mind all night. All she wanted was to be with him. But that possibility was gone. After hours of moping she had decided that the best thing to do would be to go over to Todd's house. After all, if she planned to maintain her relationship with him, she knew she had better start working at it as soon as possible.

She rang the bell, and Todd answered immediately.

He seemed surprised to see Elizabeth even though she had called to say she would be coming. *I guess I am a little early,* she thought.

"Hold on a second," Todd said nervously. He seemed to be hiding something behind his back. He closed the door partway and fumbled with something off to the side, then invited Elizabeth in.

"Sorry," he apologized. "I didn't expect you so quickly. I . . . I wasn't ready."

"What were you doing?" Elizabeth asked suspiciously.

"When?" Todd asked.

"Just now," Elizabeth elaborated. "Behind the door." Todd fidgeted a little and turned away from her.

"Oh, nothing," he said quickly, helping her to slip the windbreaker off her shoulders. Elizabeth adjusted the strap of her blue plaid cotton tank dress. She had chosen the outfit because she knew it was one of Todd's favorites and she felt guilty about not seeing him much lately.

But now that Elizabeth thought about it, she realized that Todd hadn't made an effort to see her either. A wave of insecurity swept over her. What *had* he been doing behind the door just now? What could he be hiding from her? Could there be a Devon equivalent in his life?

Elizabeth shuddered at the thoughts that ran through her mind. It had never occurred to her that Todd might be seeing someone else. Until now.

As she followed Todd into the Wilkinses' living room she realized she was actually scared. They sat down at the same time, taking seats on opposite ends of the large brown sofa. Todd stared intently at Elizabeth.

"Is there something wrong?" he asked with a worried look. Elizabeth sat silently for a moment before speaking.

"I just feel so far away from you right now," she told him, her voice quiet. Todd's large brown eyes gazed at her compassionately.

"Then come over here and get close," he replied, his voice full of warmth. Elizabeth moved over next to him, and he immediately wrapped her up in his arms. She rested on his broad chest, and he planted small, tender kisses on the top of her head. As he held her tightly she felt surrounded by his love. Elizabeth realized she had nothing to worry about. Not with Todd. But as she lay there with him a strange feeling came over her. It was clear that Todd still loved her, but she wasn't sure if she was relieved or disappointed by her realization. Being in his arms wasn't as enjoyable or as exciting as it had been before. There didn't seem to be any fireworks between them anymore.

Elizabeth was overwhelmed by a feeling of

dread. She had just sent Jessica on a date with Devon so that she could remain with Todd. *What was I thinking?* she asked herself. Elizabeth had come over to Todd's to help herself feel better, but now she was feeling worse.

Todd relaxed his hold on Elizabeth, kissing her head once more gently.

"I hate to move, but I'm going to run out to the kitchen and grab some popcorn. We can't watch the movie without some grub, can we?" Elizabeth forced a small smile as Todd got up from the sofa.

When he had left the room, Elizabeth moved forward in her seat and looked around anxiously. She was searching for a distraction, something to keep her from being alone with her thoughts. A movie case sitting on the glass coffee table caught her eye. Leaning forward, Elizabeth grabbed the box and flipped it over to see what Todd had chosen.

She read the title and sighed. *An action movie. Great,* she thought sarcastically. Todd knew that she liked classic movies, and he enjoyed them too. In fact, *Casablanca* was a favorite with both of them. But for some reason he had been on a real destruction kick lately when it came to films. He never seemed to want to get a movie unless he could be guaranteed of an explosive opening scene.

She couldn't help but think back to her discussion with Devon in chemistry class on Wednesday. *He likes old movies,* she recalled sadly. *If I hadn't been so foolish and sent Jessica out with him, I could be watching* Casablanca *with him right now.*

Elizabeth was suddenly struck by a vision of Jessica and Devon having a great time together. She could see them now. Laughing, talking, walking hand in hand down the beach. The images in her mind almost brought tears to her eyes. She tried to think of something else, but just one thought ran through her mind over and over again.

Have I made a terrible mistake?

"The air is still tonight. Good weather for setting off fireworks," Devon jested, looking at Elizabeth out of the corner of his eye.

She just sighed and nodded.

Devon couldn't shake the feeling that something wasn't right. He was walking along the beach on a starry night with the girl of his dreams, and he just didn't feel comfortable.

He had thought that once Elizabeth admitted she cared for him too, things would just fall into place. After all, in chemistry class everything had come so naturally for them. He and Elizabeth had always enjoyed excellent conversations and never experienced awkward pauses or uncomfortable silences.

But tonight was unlike any other time that they had been together. Everything felt forced. He hadn't seen Elizabeth's keen wit once. He could see her next to him, but in some strange way it didn't seem like she was really there. He felt distant from her, as though he didn't know her at all. In fact, it was as though she were a completely different person.

Maybe I just need to give it some time, be patient, Devon thought. *After all, this is the first chance we've had to be together outside of school. And Elizabeth did say she was nervous. I'm sure her situation with Todd is weighing heavily on her mind.*

He looked over at Elizabeth. She certainly was beautiful in the moonlight. He loved the way her blond hair shimmered, reflecting the glow of the moon. He squeezed her hand affectionately, and she turned to face him. Even in the darkness he could see her dazzling blue-green eyes. But as he gazed at her he experienced a strange feeling. Actually it was more like a *lack* of feeling.

"Is something wrong?" she asked, her brow furrowing.

"No, not at all," he lied, forcibly relaxing his features. He didn't want to let on that he felt totally out of sorts.

"Good," she said, smiling back at him. "I'd hate to think you weren't having a good time. It is, after all, our first date. Right?"

167

"Right," Devon agreed, attempting to sound cheerful. But he couldn't help noticing that his feelings for Elizabeth seemed to have changed completely.

Normally when he stared into Elizabeth's eyes, he felt like he could see inside her, deep into her soul. He usually connected with her effortlessly. Sometimes he felt that he could hold her gaze forever. It was as though time stood still and the world around them disappeared. But as he stared at her now, he noticed that those feelings were absent.

Devon realized that he didn't feel the special attraction that he cherished at all. It was completely gone, and in its place he felt only boredom. *Is it possible that now that I have Elizabeth, I no longer want her?* he asked himself. Devon hated to think he could be so shallow.

"So how do you like Sweet Valley so far?" Elizabeth asked.

"It seems like a really nice town," Devon answered flatly. "Did you grow up here?"

"Sure did," she answered. She continued talking, but Devon was tuning her out. *What is going on here?* he asked himself. *We're making small talk. It's like we're two strangers at some boring cocktail party!*

Devon was still struggling to make sense of his thoughts when suddenly Elizabeth stopped walking and grasped his hand more firmly. Before he could say anything, she had pulled him close and wrapped her arms around his neck. She began to kiss him forcefully.

Devon was stunned. He tried to relax and enjoy the kiss, and for a moment he was successful. It was nice to be so close to her, but then he realized he felt nothing. Her kisses left him cold.

Putting his hands on Elizabeth's shoulders, he pushed her back gently so that he could see her face. When he stared into her eyes, he saw a mischievous glint that he had never seen before. All at once everything became clear.

"Jessica?" The girl in front of him smiled widely. Devon's heart plummeted.

"I'm glad you finally noticed," she commented flirtatiously. "Now where were we?" She wrapped her arms around him again and pulled him closer.

Devon was so confused that when she started kissing him for a second time, he didn't know what to do. *What's going on here?* he wondered, unable to think. His mind was reeling from the sudden change of events. *This can't be happening,* he told himself. *It isn't right.* But even as the thought entered his mind, Jessica was pulling him closer. She ran one hand through his hair and deepened the kiss. Devon kissed back automatically, feeling almost powerless to stop. The embrace was warm, and Jessica's lips were so sweet.

She is beautiful, and she's definitely a good kisser, Devon told himself, attempting to rationalize his actions. But he could only bury his true feelings momentarily. The physical attraction began to fade, and Devon felt himself becoming angry instead.

He shoved her away and took a step backward.

"You tricked me!" he spat angrily, wiping the back of his hand across his lips. His voice was full of venom, but Jessica didn't appear to be terribly upset. She looked at him smugly, obviously amused by his reaction.

"And you didn't seem to mind too much," she said in a sultry voice, moving closer to him once again. Devon put out his hand to stop her from advancing.

"Stay away from me," he said, his voice filled with resentment. Jessica looked back at him more seriously this time, but she still didn't seem to fully understand how angry he was.

"What's your problem, Devon?" she sneered. "I'm the one you should be with. Not Liz." Then her features softened, and she touched his cheek seductively. "Besides, you seemed to enjoy kissing me. . . ." Devon was enraged. He couldn't believe her nerve.

"I could easily use you, Jessica, and then throw you away," he said bitterly. He gave his words a moment to sink in. "But that's not the way I work." The look on Jessica's face turned to one of frustrated anger.

"Did it ever occur to you that if you gave me a chance, you might not want to throw me away?" she asked, placing her hands on her hips determinedly. But her words held no meaning for Devon. He was too infuriated to even try to let her down gently.

"You're not the one I want," he said coldly. "You're not even my type." Jessica's face hardened.

"And just who is?" she asked in a huff. "Elizabeth?" Devon hesitated at the mention of her name. Before he could respond, he was cut off by Jessica's bitter laughter.

"Well, that's just too bad," she sneered. "If you don't want me, that's your loss. But for your information, Elizabeth is madly in love with Todd Wilkins. She would never give him up for you." Jessica's eyes were narrow slits full of fury. "So spend your Saturday night alone. You deserve it." Jessica turned abruptly and stormed off down the beach.

Devon was left standing alone, with only the sound of waves crashing on the shore to console him. He threw out his arms angrily and kicked the sand underneath his feet.

"How could I have been so stupid?" he chastised

himself. He was filled with rage. He realized that Elizabeth must have told Jessica to meet him there. How else would Jessica have known where to find him? He couldn't believe Elizabeth could be so low, but he was equally disgusted with himself. He had let down his guard and allowed himself to care about someone, and as usual he had been devastated.

Chapter 12

Jessica scooped a large spoonful of rum raisin ice cream into her mouth. It was eleven o'clock on Saturday night, and she was sitting alone at the round table in the Wakefield kitchen. She was still fuming over her so-called "date" with Devon.

Elizabeth must think I'm a total idiot, she thought angrily. *I can't believe she had the nerve to send me out on a date with Devon while she was leading him on. Did she really think I wouldn't figure it out?*

Jessica had been drowning her sorrows in ice cream for about half an hour, but while she'd been able to numb her heartache a bit, she hadn't been able to relieve the hostility she felt toward her sister. She was upset not only because Elizabeth had tried to trick her but also because she had neglected to let Jessica in on what was going on with Devon.

How could she withhold such vital information from her own twin? Jessica wondered.

Sure, Jessica had kept things from Elizabeth before, but that was different. This kind of stuff was completely out of character for Elizabeth. But it certainly appeared that Elizabeth wasn't the angel everyone thought she was.

Jessica shoveled another heaping spoonful of ice cream into her mouth. *Well, she's going to be sorry she messed with me,* Jessica thought. *She's way out of her league.*

Just then Jessica heard the front door open. She knew Elizabeth would see the kitchen light and come in to join her. She would be dying to find out how things had gone with Devon, and Jessica intended to tell her.

Sure enough, moments after Jessica heard the door close, Elizabeth poked her head into the kitchen. When she saw Jessica, she walked in and took a seat at the table.

"Mmmm, ice cream," she said, watching as Jessica took in another mouthful. Jessica tossed the spoon in the container and handed it to Elizabeth.

"You can have it," she said, forcing herself to smile at her twin. "I'm done."

Elizabeth began digging around with the spoon,

174

eyeing Jessica at the same time. It was obvious that Elizabeth was scrutinizing her sister's every move—trying to determine from her demeanor how things had gone with Devon. Jessica remained silent. She was determined to make her sister ask for the information.

"So how was your date?" Elizabeth finally inquired, taking a small bite.

A slight quiver in Elizabeth's voice betrayed her anxiety. Jessica put a huge smile on her face and closed her eyes dreamily.

"Fabulous," she lied, grinning blissfully. Jessica watched Elizabeth's face tense visibly. *You asked for it,* she thought.

"We had a fabulous dinner at the café," she began. "Then we took a long stroll down the beach. The stars were out, and the moon was full. . . . It was *so* romantic," she gushed, hugging herself and laughing giddily.

"We held hands and talked, and then . . ." Jessica paused for effect. She was about to twist the knife in Elizabeth's back. "We kissed passionately on the seashore, with the sound of waves crashing in the background."

Jessica closed her eyes, pretending to relive the moment. But instead of thinking of Devon, Jessica was picturing Elizabeth's face. Even with her eyes closed, Jessica could see how jealous her twin was.

She opened her eyes to meet Elizabeth's gaze.

"That's great," Elizabeth said. "I'm really happy for you." She pushed the ice cream container away from her. Elizabeth's eyes were starting to look a little glassy. It was obvious that she was fighting back tears, but Jessica didn't care. She decided to take it one step further.

"I assume you went over to Todd's," she said. Elizabeth nodded. "So how was *your* date?" Jessica asked. *Did you tell your darling Todd that you've been cheating on him?* she thought snidely.

"It was OK," Elizabeth said. It was clear that she didn't want to talk about it. Jessica decided to push a little more.

"What did you do?" she asked innocently.

Elizabeth shrugged. "Nothing, really," she answered quietly. "We just watched a movie."

"Oh, well, I guess not *every* date can be romantic," Jessica said, taking her final stab.

Elizabeth rose quickly, obviously stung. She grabbed the ice cream and returned it to the freezer, then walked back over to Jessica but didn't sit down.

"I'm pretty tired," Elizabeth said wearily, turning to leave. "I'm going up to bed."

Jessica listened to her sister's slow, heavy steps and knew that her plan had worked. When she was certain that Elizabeth had gone upstairs, Jessica went to the freezer and retrieved the ice cream. She sat down at the table and began digging in again.

"Sorry, Liz," she said quietly. "But you had that coming. We'll see how well *you* handle being deceived by your own sister."

"Where do you want the food?" Bill asked, pulling a huge picnic basket and a large cooler from the surf-mobile.

"Right over here," Todd replied, pointing to the blanket he had spread out on the sand. He and Bill had left school early and headed for the beach. They both had eighth period free on Mondays, and juniors and seniors were permitted to leave the campus by just signing out.

Bill had unloaded everything from the van while Todd searched for a good place to set up. He had already set the blanket down and picked it back up several times. But finally he seemed to have found the right spot.

"Are you sure about this?" Bill asked cautiously before bringing the food over to the blanket. "I've already moved all your stuff twice."

Todd stood back, observing the blanket in its current location. He scratched his head and moved to look at it from a different angle.

"I don't know. What do you think, Bill?" he asked, frustrated. "I keep thinking I've found the perfect spot, but then the sun seems wrong or it's too close to the water. . . . I just can't make up my mind." Bill walked over to where Todd stood and patted him firmly on the back.

"Hey, relax, man," he said. "What are you so edgy about? It's not like this is your first date with Elizabeth." Todd looked back at Bill's calm face and couldn't help laughing at himself.

"You're right," he admitted. "I know I'm being an idiot."

He dug into the sand with his foot and then looked at Bill again. "It's just that in planning this whole thing for Liz, I've realized how much she means to me," Todd said quietly. "I know it's corny, but I just want everything to be perfect for her."

"That's not corny," Bill reassured him. "But you shouldn't get yourself so worked up. I'm sure Elizabeth's going to be happy with whatever you do. You guys have been together for a long time."

Todd knew Bill was right. Elizabeth wasn't picky. She would be excited by the simple fact that Todd had remembered the one-year anniversary of her first published article. Especially since Elizabeth herself seemed to have forgotten it.

"OK, let's get set up," Todd said confidently, feeling more relaxed and upbeat. "The blanket is fine where it is."

"Absolutely perfect," Bill agreed. He brought the picnic basket over to the center of the spread and set it down. "Now let's get some of this other stuff together before Elizabeth gets here and catches you unprepared."

"Good idea," Todd replied.

He began removing items from the pile that Bill had stacked up next to the blanket. There was so much stuff, if looked like he and Bill were planning to camp out at the beach for a week.

First Todd grabbed the small platform that he planned to put their food on. It was a wooden dinner tray about three feet long and one and a half feet wide that stood ten inches off the ground. He placed the tray in the center of the blanket and then put two silver candlesticks with elegant white candles in the middle.

"That looks great," Bill said, handing him a crystal vase and a bouquet of flowers Todd had picked up at a florist's on the way.

Todd arranged the flowers in the vase and set it between the candlesticks. Together they made a beautiful centerpiece. He stood back next to Bill and looked at what they had done so far.

"Not bad," he observed proudly.

He crouched down and placed his radio at the edge of the blanket, then put in the tape of Elizabeth's favorite music so it would be ready to go when she arrived. Next he arranged her presents on one side of the table.

"Wow, you really went all out for this, didn't you?" Bill said with respect. Todd nodded modestly. He downplayed his efforts even though he knew he had indeed pushed himself to the limit to pull everything together.

I'd do anything for Elizabeth, he thought. *Nothing is too good for her.* He looked up at the sun, noticing that its position in the sky had changed quite a bit since they had arrived.

"How are we on time?" he asked Bill, beginning to get a bit nervous again.

"Relax," Bill answered, checking his watch. "We still have five minutes before school is even out. That gives you a good hour and a half to finish setting up."

"Good. Let's start on the food," he said, gesturing toward the basket and the cooler. "I just have some final touches to put on some of the dishes, and then we'll be all set. There's a hot plate in that box—" Todd was cut off by Bill's laughter.

"I don't believe it," Bill said. "You really are turning into Julia Child."

"Hey, it wasn't my idea," Todd said defensively. "Enid told me that the fo—" Todd stopped himself before he mispronounced the word. "The Italian bread would taste better if I melted the cheese and stuff on top right before eating it instead of letting it sit overnight."

"Whatever you say," Bill answered, still chuckling.

"Look, you don't need to make fun of me. I just want everything to be—"

"Yeah, I know," Bill interrupted him, "perfect."

"That's right," Todd agreed. "Perfect."

Finally this horrible day is over, Elizabeth thought as she walked slowly down the hall. *I can't believe I managed to avoid Devon and Todd all day long.*

Over the weekend Elizabeth had decided that the best thing she could do would be to lie low and avoid both Devon and Todd until she could figure out how to deal with her feelings. Thankfully, Principal Cooper had canceled first period that morning for an assembly, so Elizabeth was spared hearing all about the perfect date from Devon. It was hard enough listening to Jessica go on about it all weekend—Elizabeth didn't think she could handle hearing the same sentiments from Devon's lips. *Now all I have to do is get out of here before I bump into Todd or Devon and I'm home free,* Elizabeth thought.

But as she rounded the corner where her locker was, Elizabeth realized she wasn't safe yet. Jessica was standing at Elizabeth's locker, and Devon was standing at his, which was just a little farther down the corridor. Elizabeth groaned.

They'll probably start flirting with each other any second, Elizabeth thought ruefully. *I don't think I can take it.* She knew she would have to face them sooner or later, but Elizabeth decided she definitely preferred later. She turned quickly and began walking back the way she had come.

Maybe she could just hide out until Devon left. After all, she and Jessica were supposed to hang out this afternoon, and she doubted that Devon was planning on tagging along.

Suddenly Elizabeth heard footsteps behind her, and her heart jumped to her throat. What if Devon and Jessica had followed her? Elizabeth turned and hurried through one of the back doors, glancing once over her shoulder.

"You're acting like a big baby," she scolded herself. "You can't run from them forever." Still, a sob caught in her throat when she thought about turning back and seeing Devon and Jessica together. Elizabeth kept walking and, after a moment, realized she was heading down the trail to the field where Devon had shown her the fireworks display.

She crossed the grass and sat down by the backstop in the exact spot where she had been sitting on Friday. Dropping her books at her side, she circled her arms around her denim-clad legs and held them tightly. As she stared up at the sky she began to realize just how exhausted she was.

More than anything, she wanted to let go. She wanted to cry the tears that she had been holding back for so long. But Elizabeth was so emotionally drained, she couldn't even manage that. And she was afraid that if she did allow the tears to start flowing, she wouldn't be able to stop them.

Elizabeth closed her eyes and remembered Devon's romantic words and the touch of his fingers on her cheek.

Sweet Devon, she lamented. *He did so many wonderful things for me, and I just let him slip away.*

"Why am I always so concerned with doing the *right thing?*" Elizabeth said aloud, struggling to hold back a wave of tears. "And why does the right thing always feel so wrong lately?"

If only Devon could be here now, she thought. *He would make me feel better.* But Elizabeth wasn't sure that was true anymore. She didn't even know if Devon still cared. She'd had her chance with him, and she had blown it. Now things had changed completely. Devon was happy with Jessica, and Elizabeth was stuck with Todd—and she wasn't even certain she loved him anymore.

How did everything in my life get so messed up so quickly? she wondered, frustrated and upset.

Elizabeth pulled her knees in closer and began

to rock gently. She couldn't stand it anymore. The emotions were welling up inside her so strongly that she thought she might burst at any moment. She felt the tears spilling from her eyes and knew there was no sense in trying to stop them. This time they were coming whether she was ready for them or not.

Then suddenly she heard a twig snap behind her. Elizabeth knew she was no longer alone.

Chapter 13

Jessica waited impatiently by Elizabeth's locker. School had been out for twenty minutes already, but Elizabeth was nowhere in sight. Jessica glanced at the watch on her wrist. Only a minute had passed since the last time she had looked.

That's why I hate these things, Jessica thought, fidgeting with the uncomfortable leather strap. *The only time you ever need to look at one is when you're waiting for someone, and then it only makes the time go by more slowly.*

She loosened the closure and let the watch face slide around to the inside of her wrist. Jessica never wore a watch by choice. She didn't have a need for one. As far as she was concerned, nothing really started until she got there anyway. And she never wasted her time waiting for people. That is, never until today.

Today she had promised Todd that she would get Elizabeth to the beach on time for his big surprise. And Todd was determined to make sure she didn't mess up. He had even brought an extra watch to school and insisted she wear it so she wouldn't be late. And then he had stood by while he made her synchronize her watch to his so that he would be certain they had the same time.

It made Jessica sick to see him fussing over Elizabeth like this, especially when Elizabeth had been carrying on with Devon behind his back. *It's ironic,* Jessica thought. *Todd is worried that I'm going to ruin his surprise by getting Liz to the beach late. Meanwhile she's been flirting around with a guy she barely even knows, and now she's the one who's running behind.*

Jessica was still furious with Elizabeth for having sent her out with Devon on Saturday night. She had been completely humiliated. She knew now that he had never wanted her at all. And Elizabeth had been aware of that the whole time.

But she sent me on a date with him anyway, Jessica thought bitterly. *Of course,* Jessica recalled, smiling devilishly, *watching Elizabeth suffer all weekend while I talked about my fabulous date made things a little better.* But it hadn't been enough. Jessica was still upset. And it wasn't helping matters that she was being forced to wait around for Elizabeth now.

I should just leave and let her miss Todd's surprise, Jessica thought. *She doesn't deserve a party anyway.*

Jessica contemplated taking off and ditching Elizabeth at school, but she knew she couldn't do that. She knew Todd would be crushed. He'd be waiting at the beach all night, and Jessica certainly didn't want to hurt him. Especially after all the trouble he'd gone to putting this fabulous night together for Elizabeth.

Besides, Jessica thought, *it will serve Devon right to see Elizabeth and Todd happy together. They'll be walking around the halls tomorrow all lovey-dovey, and he'll be alone. Then he'll regret having treated me like dirt.* Jessica enjoyed imagining the look on Devon's face when he saw Elizabeth with Todd. She could hardly wait. It would be fantastic. Maybe Devon would even come running back to Jessica—begging her to give him another chance. Jessica recalled Devon's perfect body and soulful blue eyes and thought she just might consider taking him back—if he begged hard enough.

Jessica glanced at the watch again. It was now three o'clock. She had been waiting for a full thirty minutes.

Liz better get here soon, Jessica thought, *or she really is going to ruin the surprise.*

Jessica needed to get Elizabeth to the beach by four o'clock. It was a half-hour drive from the school and probably a five-minute walk from the parking lot to where Todd had set things up. She had originally planned to hang out with Elizabeth for a bit before going to the beach. After all, she had told Elizabeth they were having a sisters' night out.

Now, however, it looked like they would have to skip that part and go straight to Ocean Bay. That was fine as far as Jessica was concerned. She didn't feel like spending any more time with her sister than she had to right now.

Jessica checked her watch again. Five past three.

"You've got ten more minutes, Elizabeth Wakefield," she said to the empty corridor. "And then I'm coming after you."

Elizabeth turned to see Devon standing behind her.

A flood of emotions swept through her. She was at once excited and frightened to see him. She had wanted him to be with her, but now that he was standing just five feet away, she didn't know what to do or how to act.

Should she run up to him and pour her heart out? But what if he no longer had feelings for her? After all, he was seeing Jessica now. And Elizabeth still had to deal with Todd. She was so confused that she just sat and looked at him, unable to act. Then she noticed that he was clenching his jaw tightly. In fact, his whole body looked rigid and tense. They stared at each other for a moment without speaking. It was Devon who finally broke the silence.

"Elizabeth?" he said, a sarcastic tone coating his voice. "Or should I say Jessica? I just can't tell with you Wakefield girls these days."

"What's that supposed to mean?" Elizabeth asked, baffled.

"As if you don't know," Devon replied bitterly. He looked at her with disgust, shaking his head. But Elizabeth was still lost. Why was Devon so upset with her?

"That was a rotten thing you did, sending Jessica in your place on Saturday night," he continued, his tone icy. "I trusted you, Elizabeth."

Elizabeth opened her mouth to ask him what on earth he was talking about, but he cut her off.

"I even confided in you about my past, my parents. And then you went and betrayed me. How could you do such a thing?" he demanded.

Elizabeth was dumbstruck. She searched for the words to respond to Devon's accusations, but she was at a loss. She had thought that Devon had had a fabulous time with Jessica, but the look on Devon's face was one of pure hatred.

"But I—," Elizabeth began.

"I thought you were different," he said with contempt. "But you're just like everybody else."

Devon turned abruptly and started to walk back across the field. Elizabeth was totally confused, but she knew she had to stop him and try to explain. She sprang to her feet without thinking.

"Wait! Devon!" she called after him. He stopped where he was, but he didn't turn around to face her. Before Elizabeth knew what she was doing, the words began tumbling from her mouth.

"You have to understand. I never meant to betray you," she pleaded. "I just didn't know what else to do. I thought that if I sent Jessica to see you on Saturday instead of going myself, I could make my feelings for you disappear. I figured if you started seeing Jessica, then I'd have to put my emotions aside. That way no one would get hurt."

At these words Devon turned to face her, still standing fifteen feet away.

"But it didn't work," Elizabeth said, burying her head in her hands.

The tears had finally started flowing. She had been holding them back for so long that they came in torrents, streaming down her face. She sat down again, sobbing in the field with her knees pulled up to her chest and her arms wrapped tightly around her legs. Elizabeth felt as though she might never stop crying. Then Devon sat down next to her and put his arms around her.

"It's OK," he said soothingly, holding her tight. Elizabeth leaned into his arms. She was still crying while he comforted her, but even through her tears she could feel the incredible warmth of Devon's body against hers. When he touched her, there was an enormous surge of energy through her body—a searing heat that penetrated to her core, stirring up all her emotions but at the same time giving her a sense of peace and tranquillity. With his strong arms around her she felt completely safe and secure.

Finally her crying subsided, and she wiped away the wet tears on her face. When she felt she once again had control of herself, she looked up into Devon's slate blue eyes. He was full of compassion now, but she couldn't forget the look of fury that had been on his face a moment before.

"I still don't understand why you're so upset," she said quietly, dabbing at her eyes. "From what I heard, you and Jessica had a great time. It seems like things worked out for the best as far as you're concerned." Devon raised his eyebrows in a look of surprise.

"A good time?" he asked, his voice full of disbelief. "Is that what Jessica told you?" Elizabeth stared at him innocently. Devon laughed and shook his head.

"I thought Jessica was you when she first got there," he admitted. "But I realized the truth pretty fast. You two are nothing alike." Elizabeth was glad he noticed.

"Anyway, I confronted Jessica about it, and we had a terrible fight. We parted angrily, and that was about it. I wouldn't exactly describe it as a *good time.*" Elizabeth was stunned by his words. His account of the night was vastly different from her sister's and infinitely more believable. She heaved a heavy sigh of relief.

"So then you're not seeing Jessica?" she asked, a huge weight lifting from her shoulders.

"Of course not," Devon replied instantly, as though the thought appalled him. "I never wanted to see Jessica. It's *you* I wanted all along, Elizabeth. You're still the one I want."

Elizabeth's heart soared with happiness. She had thought she had lost Devon, that she had ruined her only chance to be with the one guy who was obviously her soul mate.

"Is what you said before true?" Devon asked. "Do you really have feelings for me too?" he asked hopefully. Elizabeth knew she couldn't deny it any longer.

"I always have," she conceded. "From the first time we touched." She felt herself blush furiously at her confession but continued anyway. "I just didn't know what to do about it. I feel drawn to you with every ounce of my being. Sometimes the connection is so strong, it scares me," she said breathlessly.

"I know," Devon told her, cupping her chin in his hand and turning her face toward his. "Sometimes it scares me too," he confided. "But what scares me even more is the thought of not being with you." Elizabeth gazed into his tumultuous blue eyes and felt herself beginning to drown in their swirling depths.

"You need to listen to your heart, Elizabeth," he told her. "Stop trying to rationalize everything. You can't fight something this powerful, this natural."

His voice was only a whisper, yet every word echoed in Elizabeth's ears. There was no way she could hold back this time. Her heart was pounding in her chest so hard that she could hear it, and her skin tingled in anticipation.

When Devon finally pressed his lips to hers, she felt the intensity of his kiss throughout her body. And without a moment's hesitation Elizabeth locked her arms tightly around his neck and kissed him back.

"That's it," Jessica said, checking her watch one last time. "I'm through standing around."

If it weren't for Todd waiting at the beach,

you'd be walking home, sis, Jessica thought as she stormed down the hallway.

The school was more or less deserted at this point. Everyone had either gone home or to their various sporting practices or club meetings. Jessica would much rather be at cheerleading than tracking down her sister, but she had canceled practice in order to do this favor for Todd. *Mainly because I thought Elizabeth was helping me with Devon,* she thought bitterly. *What a laugh.*

The first place Jessica decided to check was the *Oracle* office. She walked in and looked around, but it was just as deserted as the corridor. She found Mr. Collins sitting at the desk in his private office.

"Hello, Jessica," he greeted her as she knocked lightly on his door. "Can I help you with something?"

"I'm looking for Elizabeth," she said plainly. "Have you seen her?"

"Not since class today," Mr. Collins answered. His handsome face grew concerned. "Is something wrong, Jessica? You seem upset, and I noticed Elizabeth wasn't feeling well today either." Jessica knew he was trying to be polite, and his concern was genuine, but she was in a hurry.

"No, everything's fine," she answered quickly, turning to go. "I'm just late for something. Thanks, Mr. Collins."

Jessica rushed down the corridor and out the back door. She found a group of kids playing Frisbee and figured it wouldn't hurt to try them.

"Hey, have you guys seen Liz?" she asked, her frustration reflected in her voice.

"She went down the trail to the softball field about a half hour ago," Caroline Pearce answered. "She had her books and everything, and—" The tall redhead tended to be long-winded, so Jessica cut her off.

"Thanks, Caroline," she said, speeding off down the trail. Jessica knew she had to hurry. If she found Elizabeth now and they left right away, they would only be about five minutes late. Then she could be done with this whole mess and ditch Todd's stupid watch too.

As Jessica reached the bottom of the trail she looked through the trees and noticed movement on the other side of the field.

Finally, she thought. *Tomorrow, when I'm done playing nice and getting Elizabeth to the beach on time, I'm going to kill her for putting me through this.*

Jessica stepped into the clearing and froze in her tracks.

She felt her heart clench in anger and her stomach turned so quickly, she felt as if she might throw up.

Elizabeth was indeed there, sitting on the opposite side of the field. But she wasn't alone.

She was locked in a passionate embrace with Devon Whitelaw.

Jessica stood, dumbfounded for a moment, unable to move. Elizabeth and Devon were so wrapped up in each other that they didn't even notice Jessica's presence.

I can't believe this, Jessica thought frantically. *This can't really be happening.* Jessica rubbed her eyes, but the vision didn't disappear. What did Elizabeth think she was doing? Sweet, responsible, everyone's-perfect-angel Elizabeth? And Devon? Right here in broad daylight? *I guess he won't be begging for my forgiveness anytime soon,* she thought ruefully.

As quickly as she had entered the clearing Jessica turned and ran back up the trail, tears springing to her eyes.

Jessica Wakefield, you'd better have a good explanation for this, Todd thought, straightening his soft, pale blue cotton shirt and running one hand through his hair. He fiddled with the leather belt on his chinos and gazed toward the parking area by the beach entrance.

It seemed like a lifetime had passed since he had told Bill to go ahead and leave so that he would be alone when Elizabeth arrived. Todd was ready to kill Jessica. After all the hard work he had done trying to create a perfect night for Elizabeth, Jessica was going to ruin it.

I can't believe how selfish she is, Todd thought. After everything Elizabeth had done for Jessica, the girl couldn't even do this one small thing in return. He knew he never should have trusted Jessica with such an important task. After all, she wasn't exactly the most reliable person in the world.

Todd looked at the spread he had set up for Elizabeth. He had tasted the food earlier, and everything had come out perfectly, thanks to Enid's tips. He had waited until a quarter to four to put the last layer of whipped cream on the chocolate raspberry trifle so that it would look fresh. But now it was starting to look as though it had been sitting in the sun for too long. And the cheese that he had melted onto the focaccia at the last minute was now cold and hard.

Maybe I should just call Elizabeth and get her out here myself, he thought. At least then he could give her the presents. They still looked fine. And they would be able to enjoy the music and drink a toast with the sparkling apple cider he had brought. The night could still be salvaged.

Todd was just about to give up on Jessica and call the Wakefield house when he saw Elizabeth coming over the dunes. He breathed a sigh of relief. *Thank goodness,* he thought. *Maybe now we can get this party under way.* But as she got closer he realized it wasn't Elizabeth, but Jessica. Todd's anger returned. By the time she reached him, he was absolutely raging.

"Where's Elizabeth?" he asked furiously. "I asked you to do one simple thing, just get Elizabeth to the beach on time, and—" He stopped in midsentence. Jessica's face was streaked with tears, and she was still crying. Todd was baffled. What on earth was going on? But before he could ask, Jessica burst out angrily.

"You want to know where your precious Elizabeth is?" she sneered. Todd didn't know how to respond, but it didn't matter. He didn't have time to. Jessica was positively furious, and she was ranting hysterically.

"I'll tell you where she is," Jessica hissed. "While you've been working so hard to celebrate Elizabeth and her stupid article, she's been deceiving both of us!"

Todd had no idea what Jessica was talking about, but she *was* given to dramatics. He hoped she was simply overreacting about something.

"What is it, Jess? What's the matter?" Todd demanded.

"Everything!" Jessica spat. Her face hardened,

198

and a terrible feeling settled in the pit of Todd's stomach.

"Your beloved, loyal Elizabeth is at this very moment in the field behind the high school, joined at the lip with Devon Whitelaw!"

Thrown into a jealous rage, Todd just wants to make Devon Whitelaw go away. But Devon isn't about to give up his new love without a fight. How far will Todd and Devon go to win Elizabeth's heart? Find out in Sweet Valley High #139, **Elizabeth Is Mine**.

Bantam Books in the Sweet Valley High series
Ask your bookseller for the books you have missed

SIGN UP FOR THE SWEET VALLEY HIGH® FAN CLUB!

Hey, girls! Get all the gossip on Sweet Valley High's® most popular teenagers when you join our fantastic Fan Club! As a member, you'll get all of this really cool stuff:

- Membership Card with your own personal Fan Club ID number
- A Sweet Valley High® Secret Treasure Box
- Sweet Valley High® Stationery
- Official Fan Club Pencil (for secret note writing!)
- Three Bookmarks
- A "Members Only" Door Hanger
- Two Skeins of J. & P. Coats® Embroidery Floss with flower barrette instruction leaflet
- Two editions of *The Oracle* newsletter
- Plus exclusive Sweet Valley High® product offers, special savings, contests, and much more!

Be the first to find out what Jessica & Elizabeth Wakefield are up to by joining the Sweet Valley High® Fan Club for the one-year membership fee of only $6.25 each for U.S. residents, $8.25 for Canadian residents (U.S. currency). Includes shipping & handling.

Send a check or money order (do not send cash) made payable to "Sweet Valley High® Fan Club" along with this form to:

SWEET VALLEY HIGH® FAN CLUB, BOX 3919-B, SCHAUMBURG, IL 60168-3919

NAME _____
(Please print clearly)

ADDRESS _____

CITY_____ STATE _____ ZIP_____
(Required)

AGE _____ BIRTHDAY_____ /_____ /_____

Offer good while supplies last. Allow 6-8 weeks after check clearance for delivery. Addresses without ZIP codes cannot be honored. Offer good in USA & Canada only. Void where prohibited by law.
©1993 by Francine Pascal   LCI-1383-123